JOE WELLER
EXPLORES
HAUNTED HOTEL

AN EXPLORING
HAUNTED &
ABANDONED
BOOK

JOE WELLER
EXPLORES

HAUNTED HOTEL

HEADLINE

First published in 2017
by HEADLINE PUBLISHING GROUP

1

Cataloguing in Publication Data is available from the British Library

Hardback ISBN 978 1 4722 5263 0

Design by Amazing15
Photographs on pages 2, 7, 8, 12, 17, 27, 37, 40, 44, 46, 50, 59 (top), 67, 71, 75, 77, 79, 80, 83,
88, 89, 94, 107, 108, 118, 119, 121, 122, 125, 127, 133, 136, 139, 147, 148, 155, 156, 159, 160,
195, 201, 204, 209, 216, 218, 222, 223, 242, 244, 253, 254, 255, 256 by Justin de Souza, all
other photography courtesy of Shutterstock.
Printed and bound in Germany by Mohn Media

Headline's policy is to use papers that are natural, renewable and recyclable products and
made from wood grown in sustainable forests. The logging and manufacturing processes are
expected to conform to the environmental regulations of the country of origin.

HEADLINE PUBLISHING GROUP
An Hachette UK Company
Carmelite House
50 Victoria Embankment
London EC4 0DZ

www.headline.co.uk
www.hachette.co.uk

SAFETY NOTE

All the characters and the events in this book are entirely fictional and the dodgy escapades I get up to in this book are a product of my imagination. Please don't trespass on private property or re-enact any of the scenes in this book as some of them are illegal or dangerous. I don't want you getting into trouble, boys and girls!

INTRODUCTION

So this is it! After going on some of the most dodgy explorations, I have made my own Haunted & Abandoned exploring story...

There are so many different things that can happen – or even go wrong – when filming these exploring videos, yet only certain things actually occur. My issue was, I'd had so many mental ideas that would make for a sick video, yet would be impossible to make happen when filming. Through creating this book I finally have had the chance to put them all into one place! What's more, I wanted to make it an interactive novel so that you, the viewer, can't rely on me to lead the way anymore… It's down to you now!

I hope you enjoy it, guys. This is certainly a very dodgy experience you're about to embark on, but it's been so much fun creating it this year. Good luck you young boys and girls and others!

PROLOGUE

riory Grange Hotel. Look at it sat there, all dark stone and shadows and cobwebs. Dead. Maybe. According to the sign that still hangs at the end of the driveway, this place once had five stars. You can see them right there on the chipped paint sign, next to the graffiti and the explosive stain of what you're really hoping is just a ball of earth, thrown at the sign by bored kids.

Online the reviews were a different story:

This place is supposed to be luxurious, but the noise at night! We couldn't sleep because of the row coming from the room next door. Called management and they actually had the cheek to insist there was nobody staying in that room! As if we hadn't been listening to them for hours! Crying, shouting and shifting the furniture. We won't be staying there again.

Given the cost of the room, you'd hope they could afford heating. My wife and I just couldn't get warm.

Staff are useless! I needed help with my door lock and I saw a porter further along the hallway. I called to him but he just stared at me then walked off! I went after him but when I turned the corner he'd gone! He'd actually run off rather than help me!

And on, and on, and on.

There were good reviews too. Of course there were. A place like this wouldn't stay in business for a month, let alone ten years, if it was always that bad. But the number of bad reviews grew and the number of guests didn't.

And it wasn't just the reviews. After all, not all of the guests survived long enough to write one.

And then, finally, there was the fire. And the screaming. And the smothering smoke.

So now it sits there. Dead. Maybe.

You can't tell the difference between the gardens and the woods that surround them. It's all just green. Brambles like barbed wire, nettles grown thick into hedges. Piles of dead leaves under your feet, dry and brittle on top, wet and rotten underneath. Like walking on dead bodies.

The driveway is a scar amongst the foliage, leading up to the tall brick wall that surrounds this place like a prison. The only thing new here are signs telling you to 'Keep Out'. There are so many of them it feels like a warning about much more than the fact the property is private. It feels like someone is screaming at you to run.

Beyond this wall the grounds of the hotel begin.

To one side there's a maze. A dark cube of overgrown hedges. Once people got lost here, now the maze itself seems confused as to what it should do.

A few metres away, buried under ivy, there's a mound of stone. It used to be a fountain. Now it's just big, discoloured squares of rock, like rotten teeth. Maybe it died of thirst. Water's not run through its pipes for decades. The hotel owners planned to maintain it but the cost was too high. So they left it as a bit of decorative lawn art for the guests to take pictures of. It looked good on the brochures. Classy. Ancient.

The last time the fountain drank, Priory Grange was a private home, lived in by the Godling family. Rich, famous, broken.

Isaac Godling. Gentleman, millionaire, bastard. When you want to poison a tree you pour the poison at its roots. Same with a family.

Isaac was toxic and those that came after him – or came close to him – soon began to feel it.

But maybe the roots go back further than Isaac and his ruined family. Maybe the roots stretch all the way back to when there really was a priory here rather than just a building named after one. Maybe it's because of the monks and the things the villagers believed they did here. Maybe they scarred the place. Because sometimes the earth remembers. Sometimes, it doesn't matter what you build, how much you try and change, deep down beneath it all, the place is just broken. The place is haunted.

Looking up at the towering, dark shadow of the Priory Grange Hotel (dead, maybe) you can well believe it.

'Right then,' says Joe, 'we going in or what?'

START AT NUMBER 1, AND LET'S HOPE YOU GET THROUGH THIS THING ALIVE.

'So, here we go! Abandoned hotel. The boys have come to explore.' Joe's face is lit by the camera light, a pure white beam that kills the night. 'We're stood in the grounds of what used to be the Priory Grange Hotel. Pretty pricey place to stay at. It closed, like, a year ago and since then it's just been sat here caught up in some dodgy ownership battle. Turns out the company that owned it hadn't paid their mortgage so the bank wanted to take it from them. So nobody's been allowed in here. It's basically just been left – with everything still inside. Now the bank has sold it on and they're going to build flats or something. People are coming in to strip the place before the bulldozers level it all. They're literally turning up tomorrow morning so this is the last night to do this. Another couple of weeks and this'll just be mud and rubble.'

'Sounds good,' you reply. Because, honestly? You already don't like the feel of this place. Being here is freaking you out and the idea of broad daylight and a bulldozer tearing its way through all of this is no bad thing.

'And for once we've actually been able to get permission,' he says. 'Cos someone at the bank likes the videos and was able to get us in.'

'That's decent!' you say.

'Just is! But anyway, we have the keys to the gate and the night is young, so let's take a look.'

You start walking towards the building.

'This literally looks so dodgy,' says Joe, 'but I guess nobody cares, or they didn't want to spend the money on repairing it.'

'The fire?' you ask.

'Yeah,' he nods. 'The fire. The hotel wasn't doing well anyway, lots of weird stuff happening which I'll tell you about in a bit, but then a fire broke out – or someone started it, nobody really knows – and that

'They really don't want people getting in here do they?' you say.

'There's probably some valuable stuff inside,' Joe replies.

A big metal gate has been constructed over the entrance. Joe unlocks the padlock on the gate and you step through. He locks the gate again behind him and puts the keys in his pocket.

'Look after those,' you tell him, 'I don't want to get stuck in here until the morning.'

'They're safe,' he says, patting his pocket, and the two of you head up the driveway.

You can't get a full sense of the place in the dark, just the small circle that's visible in the halo of your light. Old lawns, once immaculate squares bordered with plant beds, are now long messes of green, like someone had painted a garden and then swirled their finger through it while the paint was still wet. On your left, the old fountain. On your right a statue of an angel, stone wings spread, ready to take off and get the hell out of there. Sensible angel.

Ahead of you the building rears up, blocking out the night sky. It's huge, a gothic castle, a place taken right out of a horror movie. The old stone is stained and blackened with dirt and soot, some of the windows shattered and filthy.

The driveway opens out into a forecourt of weed-strewn gravel. On your right, a huge stone porch, an umbrella of shadow hiding the front door.

'Hang about,' says Joe, before announcing to anything that can hear: 'We come in peace, we mean no disrespect to any spirits that may be here.' He stands there for a minute: 'Alright then! What do you reckon? Try the front door or circle around the building and check the outside first?'

FRONT DOOR? GO TO NUMBER 8.

MOVE AROUND THE HOUSE? GO TO NUMBER 5.

It was the noise that was doing Scott Monroe's head in. Such a tiny noise. Nothing really. The sort of thing that most days you wouldn't even notice. But today… tonight… the buzzing of that fly made him want to scream. If he could just get to sleep then it would be fine but it had been hours now, hours of staring at the ceiling and listening to the sound of that horrible winged bastard buzzing around the room.

It wasn't the fly. He knew that really. His head was too full, that was all. He just couldn't switch off.

Ed Leonard. It would all have been fine if it wasn't for Ed Leonard.

Ed Leonard with his expensive haircut, his expensive car, his big perfect grin. During these long sleepless nights – because tonight really wasn't the first – Scott liked to imagine spending five minutes with that grin and a hammer. Not a big hammer, no, one of those little ones for knocking in tacks. Just big enough to take out one perfect bloody tooth at a time. What a happy five minutes that would be.

Ed Bloody Leonard.

If it hadn't been for him, Scott wouldn't be lying here on his own tonight. Or any night. Hannah would be lying here with him. Just as it should be.

It had been going on a while. He and Hannah had gone out for drinks after work a few times, and then recently they'd started meeting for dinner. The new Thai place near the train station, or the Japanese under the arches. It had never led to anything, they hadn't even kissed. Honestly? Scott had never quite had the nerve. They'd had some good nights. They always had a laugh. In a way, Scott had been scared of pushing his luck. Because if he'd tried it on and she'd said no then he'd have broken it wouldn't he? And it just felt too lovely to break. So he had settled for a hug and a peck on the cheek as she got in a minicab.

Instead Scott waited. One day, he was sure, she'd make a move, and then that would be that and everything would be alright. Yes.

No.

Because he'd been emailed this offer for a one-night stay in a lovely hotel in the country. He'd nearly deleted it. Ever since he'd been persuaded to book a 'romantic weekend' with his ex he'd been getting spam emails for meals in restaurants, hotel breaks, train tickets. Usually he just binned them but that day, bored in the office, he'd glanced at it and the hotel looked so posh and the price was so cheap…

'Why Pay More?' it had said. 'Book Now.'

So he had. 'Well,' he thought, 'now we'll know won't we?' He was seeing Hannah that night anyway so he thought he'd spring it on her as a surprise. He might say he'd been given it free through work or something. So as not to look too pushy if she freaked out about the idea of sharing a room with him. But she wouldn't, would she? Surely he hadn't been reading the signals that wrong? She liked him, he knew she did – and he could always book another separate room. It would still be a nice weekend break. There was loads of stuff to do at the hotel, it looked great. There were even trips you could book, horse riding would be good he decided. He'd actually been on a horse once, at Scout camp, and it hadn't thrown him or anything. He could probably impress her with that.

So they were on their second bottle of wine, everything was great, laughing, happy, perfect. Then he mentioned it.

'Oh,' her face had fallen, 'I can't that weekend I'm afraid. Ed's taking me to Boomtown.'

'Ed?'

'You know, Ed Leonard from marketing?' she smiled bashfully, 'we've sort of being seeing each other.'

What? Wait… WHAT?

'Seeing each other?'

'Yeah, I didn't want to mention it because I don't want to jinx it. Can't your boyfriend go with you?'

Boyfriend? BOYFRIEND?

There then followed the most embarrassing half hour of his life. Hannah had thought he was gay. She'd thought they were just seeing each other as friends. She thought he was actually in a relationship with his flatmate Dan – who *was* gay. Now Scott thought about it, there had been that time when Dan had joked about how Scott was the perfect boyfriend because, 'He always does my washing, he's always here to prop me up when I feel low and, best of all, never minds me seeing other guys!' It had been a joke. Just a stupid joke. Oh God. All this time and… OH GOD.

He'd done his best to laugh it off. In fact, he was so embarrassed he almost did pretend he was in a relationship with Dan because then, at

least, he wouldn't have had to admit that he'd been asking her to come away with him because he really wanted them to…

Shit. He could have just crawled under the table and died.

So now she was enjoying her festival with Ed Bloody Leonard and he was enjoying his oh-so-grown-up weekend break. For one. Because he'd paid for it – including the horse-riding trip – and it turned out you didn't get a penny back if you cancelled. He'd thought it would be fine, coming on his own. Maybe even quite nice. And yes, for about five minutes he'd had this amazing daydream about meeting some babe in the hotel bar and, 'Oh my God! This is so amazing, and to think, I nearly didn't come!'

There had been nobody in the hotel bar.

Nobody at all.

No wonder they were practically giving the rooms away.

They'd even cancelled the horse riding due to 'veterinary difficulties'.

So now he was lying here in his boring bed, and the only company he had to share it with kept flying around his face.

The fly landed on his nose.

'That's it!' Scott screamed, whipping back the bed covers and reaching for the light switch.

He was going to kill that bloody fly. He was going to spread it all over the wall.

He turned all the lights on, padding around the floor, head turning left and right, trying to catch sight of the fly. He grabbed his *Classic Cars* magazine – he was determined to own a Lotus Elise one day – and curled it into a tube.

'Going to beat the shit out of you,' he said, then caught sight of himself in the mirror. Naked, overweight, a magazine in his hand, stood there talking to flies.

He bet Ed Bloody Leonard never had to talk to flies.

It buzzed past him and he lashed out with the magazine but it was no good, he'd have to wait for it to land on something. You couldn't just swat flies out of thin air, you had to sneak up on them while they were sat on stuff, doing whatever it was flies did when they weren't annoying you. Rubbing their horrible little faces with their stupid little legs.

He couldn't hear it. Did that mean it had landed? He thought it probably did.

He slowly moved around the room, checking the surfaces. The lampshades, the desk, the bed, the really stupid uncomfortable chair that every hotel room always has sat in a corner of it. He couldn't see it anywhere.

And then… there it was, perched on the edge of the waste bin.

He stared at it for a second, worried that if he moved he'd scare it off.

Slowly, so, so slowly… he took a couple of steps towards the bin.

'Don't you go anywhere you horrible bastard,' he muttered raising the magazine above his head and trying to perfect his aim.

The fly flew away.

He felt like screaming.

He probably could scream. Not like there was anyone in this place to complain about the noise. Not that he could tell anyway. Although, now he came to think about it, it seemed he could hear voices coming through the wall from the room next door. Distracted for a moment he moved to the wall and put his ear to it. Yes, definitely voices.

'Someone likes old rides,' said a male voice.

'You should introduce them to your mum,' says another.

What was that all about?

Then the fly buzzed past him again and he forgot all about the voices, spinning away from the wall and chasing after the fly. It was heading for the bathroom.

Again he caught his reflection in the mirror, just out of the corner of his eye this time, and his brain didn't quite register what he was seeing because a little voice inside his head said, 'That wasn't you, the man in the mirror there, it wasn't you! He was older, thin, with a nose like a bloody pelican, a huge thing you could hang your coat off.'

But he didn't pay attention to that voice. Because of the fly. Because the fly really had to die.

He ran into the bathroom and that was a mistake. His foot landed on the mat in front of the sink and it slipped on the tiled floor. He spun, skated backwards a little way, the edge of the bath kicking his legs out from underneath him. He toppled back into it.

Thunk.

What the hell had that noise been? It had sounded bad. Like a wooden log being split open by an axe. Had he broken something? Oh God, had his clumsiness smashed one of the fittings? They'd charge him for that. Some cheap weekend break this would turn out to be.

He'd have to take a look. In a minute. He couldn't quite move right now, most of him lying in the bath, his legs dangling over the side. Was the tap running? Warm water was pooling around the back of his head.

He glanced at the tap. It was dripping, but not with water. Was that blood? It looked like blood. And there was stuff stuck on the end of the tap too, a lump of something wet with what looked like hair growing out of it.

Some hotel this was, leaving its bathrooms in such a state.

He looked up and he could see his reflection in the bathroom mirror. Actually, no he couldn't, not from this angle, of course he couldn't. What he could see was the same face he'd glimpsed before, the old, thin guy with the big nose.

Scott opened his mouth to ask the man what he was doing here but found he couldn't think of the words. It didn't matter, he could see the man wasn't actually in the room anyway. Just the mirror. How strange.

The hot water was getting very thick around his head now and the light was fading. He wondered what was going on.

He figured it out just as the light faded completely. 'Banged your head on the tap,' he thought as his world went dark.

The last thing he heard was the fly landing in the pool of blood right next to his left ear.

It began to drink.

GO TO 40.

3

'Yeah, not like we've got much choice is it?' you say and both of you get into the lift.

For all Joe's pretending it's fine, you can tell by the way he steps inside that he's not sure. Both of you enter as if you're stepping on thin ice. The cabin sinks slightly as you climb aboard, a soft creak from the cables and, just for a minute you're thinking this was a mistake. But the door is closing and there's no way you're backing out now.

The lift is holding and there's really no sign of damage. A soft, slightly orange light in the ceiling shows your reflections in the mirrors on either side of you.

When the fire broke out, the guests probably all knew to avoid using the lift so it would have sat behind its fireproofed door on whichever floor it had been left on, waiting out the flames. If the major damage really was restricted to this part of the building you might well be doing the best thing. But do you keep exploring or do you use it to go down now, to get back to safe, known territory?

Joe points the camera at the control panel. 'So, mate, what do you want to do? We could just go right back down again. Or we could go up as high as possible, where the damage might be a lot less.' An idea occurs to him. 'Or we check out what was going on on the third floor! See if there really is someone up there.'

LET'S GO BACK DOWNSTAIRS. GO TO 21.

IF WE'RE DOING THIS, LET'S GO ALL THE WAY. FOURTH FLOOR. GO TO 29.

LET'S SEE WHAT'S HAPPENING ON THE THIRD FLOOR. GO TO 15.

J oe opens the book and starts to read.

'"Spirits of the other, the hallowed realm beyond our mortal earth, we come to you in a state of honest supplication, hearts open to the light of your divine presence."'

'Sounds romantic.'

'Shush! "It is with respect and honour that we approach. Talking to you through the veil of consciousness. From our flesh to your spirit. Our breath to your stillness."'

There is a slight scuttling noise from behind you both. Something moving in the darkness.

'Did you hear that?' you ask, holding still, 'I swear something moved over there.'

'I didn't hear it,' he says, 'you serious?'

'Of course I'm serious. I'm telling you something moved.'

'Like what?'

'I don't know do I? It's pitch black in here.'

He rolls his eyes. 'I mean, like, was it a big thing or… I don't know, like a mouse or something?'

'It was something small,' you admit, 'could have been a mouse I suppose. Or a rat.'

Both of you stay perfectly still for a few seconds. There's silence.

'Well,' says Joe, 'whatever it is, it's not moving now. Let's carry on.'

'Do we have to?'

'Mate, the whole point of this spell, or whatever, is to make friends with the spirit world, that's not a bad thing is it?'

'I suppose not.'

'So it's better to finish it. The worst thing we're doing here is showing respect.'

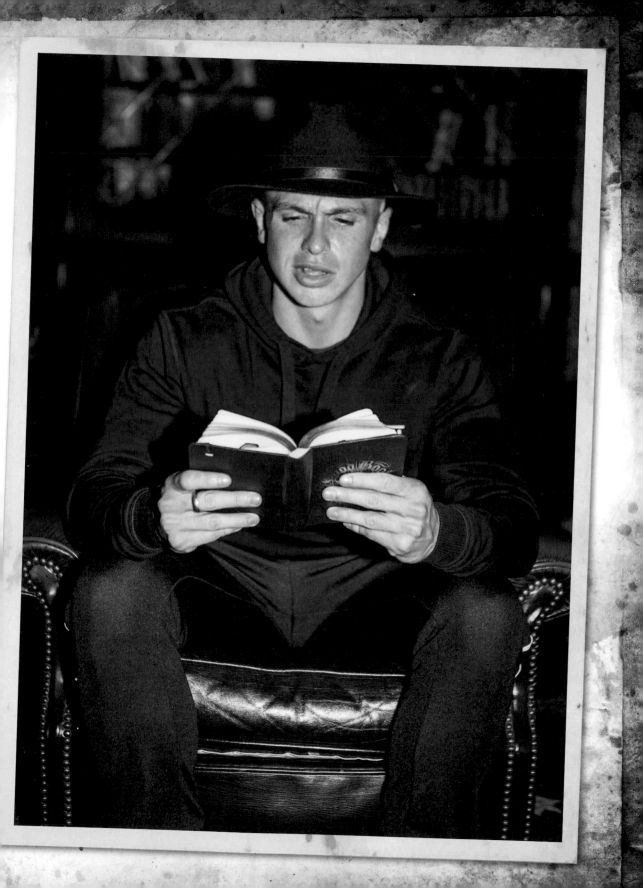

You can't really argue with that. 'OK.'

Joe finds his place and starts reading again. '"Across the worlds we make our promise, to revere your works, to mark your memory and to honour your name."'

The noise again, closer now.

'There. You hear it that time?'

'I didn't mate, you sure you're not imagining it?'

'Seriously?' You can't believe this. Is he just winding you up? Surely he heard that? It was so close! 'Check the video if you don't believe me. Something's moving around in here.'

'Like I said, probably a mouse or something. Don't start freaking out about mice.'

'Like you do about bees?'

'That's different. Bees sting. What's a mouse going to do? Steal ya sandwiches? Now shut up will you? I've nearly finished.' He starts reading again. '"So let us make peace across the Vale of Death. Share this space in harmony and mutual understanding. We reach out our hands to touch yours…"'

The lights on both of the cameras switch off.

'Jesus!' you shout. 'What the fuck's going on here?'

'I don't know,' says Joe, and he's not so relaxed now. How could he be? 'Let me check the cameras…'

You grab his arm. 'And step outside the pentagram?'

'It's only a laugh, it doesn't really mean anything…' He doesn't sound convinced and that's good because neither are you.

The noise again. The tiny patter of something on the floorboards.

'You hear it now, yeah?' you ask.

'Yeah.'

'Still think it's a mouse?'

'Well, it does kind of sound like one.'

The sound again, and he's right, it does, but that's not enough to make the panic go away because what about the lights? 'A mouse didn't turn the frigging cameras off, Joe.'

'I know… Look, I don't know what's going on, alright? What do you want me to say?'

'Nothing, you don't have to say anything! I'm just saying I'm freaked out, y'know?'

'You and me both mate.' He turns on his torch, the light shining up into your panicked faces. He aims the beam into the darkness, moving in a slow circle. The room appears slowly, washed out and grey. The bookshelves, the chairs, the cameras on their little stands. Everything appears normal. The room is empty.

Except… what's that there?

'Bring the light back this way.' You grab his arm and pull it back in the opposite direction. It falls on the back of an armchair. You squint, trying to be sure.

'What?' asks Joe. Then… 'Oh Jesus.'

He's seen it too. Because on the arm of that chair, just visible because it's at a slight angle to you, isn't that a hand?

'Tell me you see that's a hand,' you whisper. And now you wonder if that noise wasn't the sound of mice feet tapping along the floorboards at all but actually the sound of fingernails tapping on the old leather arm of a chair.

Suddenly the torch cuts out and the minute it's dark again you hear the noise. This time you can't picture anything else but old, yellow nails, long nails, nails that have grown and grown to form ugly, jagged talons. Nails tapping on leather.

'Turn it back on!' you say.

Joe's shaking the torch. 'Sorry, sorry… don't know why it's not working.' Suddenly the torch comes on again and he points it towards the chair. That shape is still there on the leather arm. Is it a hand? Surely it's a hand.

'Hang about,' says Joe, confidence creeping back into his voice again for a second. Then, before you can stop him he's running across the room to the light switches.

'Joe!' you shout.

Then the lights come flooding on and your realise that shape on the arm of the chair is part of the strap from your rucksack. You dumped the bag in the chair earlier.

'Christ,' you sigh, 'my heart is pounding.'

'Tell me about it,' he says, picking up the bag and waving the strap at you while making spooky noises. 'It seriously looked like a hand though didn't it?'

'Yeah it did.'

You walk over to another chair and sit down in it. 'That freaked me out mate, I mean properly freaked me right out.'

'You saying you want to get out of here?'

'No, I'm not saying that,' though you kind of do, 'just admitting I was bricking it, that's all.'

Joe walks over to the cameras. 'What happened to these then?'

He picks one up. 'No way.'

'What?'

'It's completely out of power. Which just isn't possible, I charged them both before we came.' He picks up the other camera. 'This is exactly the same. Both had hours of battery left in them. How does that even make sense?'

'It doesn't,' you reply, 'and it's not just that. How can both run out of power at exactly the same time?'

He just shakes his head. He goes over to his rucksack, pulls out a charging cable and his laptop. He looks around the room. 'May as well plug it in,' he says, running the laptop charge cable to the closest wall socket, plugging it in then connecting the cameras. The charging light on both starts to glow red then immediately turns green.

'See,' he says, 'both fully charged, as they should be, we've hardly used them.' He shakes his head. 'It doesn't make sense, they'd better not be knackered, it's not like we can come back another time if we don't get the footage is it?'

'Do you want to check what we've already got?' you ask him. You're wondering if maybe one of the cameras saw something just before they both turned off. If maybe, just maybe, there's an answer right there in the footage.

He thinks for a moment then decides against it. 'No, let's leave it for now. We've got a lot more left to see.'

He disconnects the cameras and checks them, they're both working fine. He hands them to you while he packs away the rest of his stuff.

'Come on then,' he says, stepping back out into the corridor, 'I don't think there's any point in hanging around in here. It's just a library.'

'With a mouse in it,' you add, because you really hope that a mouse is all it was.

'With a mouse in it,' he agrees. 'I don't think anything important happened here.'

GO TO 24.

'Let's walk around a bit first,' you suggest, 'and get an idea of the place.'

'Yeah, I think you're right,' Joe agrees, 'look through a few windows, make sure there aren't any nutters hiding out here with knives.'

'Why would there be any nutters with knives?'

'Why wouldn't there be?' He grins. 'They're probably watching us right now!'

'Shut up Joe.'

He puts on a funny voice and starts cackling. 'Watch out you little bastards! I'm gonna shank you up and take you to the cheese grater factory!' he says, waving an imaginary knife.

You move past the main entrance, following a terrace surrounding the house. You approach a large window, the light of the moon blasting back at you from the filthy glass.

'Can you see anything in there?' Joe asks, pushing his face against the window.

'Nah,' you admit, 'glass is too dirty.'

You keep moving, heading around the corner of the house.

Suddenly, a light from inside the building stops both of you in your tracks.

'Jesus!' whispers Joe, 'there's someone in there!'

Both of you duck down beneath the lit window and listen. It's completely silent.

'There can't be anyone here,' whispers Joe, 'you saw the wall, the barbed wire, the gate… the only way you get in here is with the key and we've got that.'

'How do you know someone else hasn't got one?' you ask. 'Maybe the people who are coming to clear it out are checking the place over before they start tomorrow.'

'If anyone else was going to be here, the bloke from the bank would have told me.'

'And another thing,' you add, 'how come there's power? Is the electricity supposed to be working?'

'No idea mate,' Joe admits. 'Maybe it's been reconnected for when the work starts?'

That sort of, almost, makes sense. Not quite, but you decide to go with it because as explanations go it's nice and normal and boring and safe.

You both slowly peer over the window ledge, trying to see inside. The window's so dirty the light is only coming out in vague patches.

'Was that somebody moving?' you ask, sure you just saw something shift on the other side of the dirty glass.

'Can't see anything,' Joe admits.

That movement again and a vague shape, you stare at the glass and for a second you see your own face staring out at you. Then you realise it must be a reflection.

Suddenly the light cuts out again. You listen for any sound but everywhere is as quiet as it was before.

'Maybe the power's just playing up?' you ask. 'Coming on and off. You'd think if there had been people in there moving around we'd have heard them.'

'Maybe,' says Joe.

'Anyway,' you add, 'what the hell are we panicking for? We're allowed to be here!'

'Oh yeah!' He grins. 'I'd sort of forgotten that.'

'Of course, if it's someone that's *not* allowed to be here,' you point out, 'they're not going to like us prowling around are they?'

'It's alright,' says Joe, putting on the sort of voice you'd use to talk to a baby, 'if someone tries to get you I'll keep you safe. Don't worry about any bad men, OK?'

'Piss off,' you say, smiling, 'you'll be halfway up the path running and screaming if we do see anyone. Admit it.'

There's no sound now and you're all but convinced the electrics were just playing up.

You both get up and carry on moving along the terrace.

'Stop!' says Joe, turning the light off and grabbing your arm. You both stand still a second.

'What?' you whisper.

'I swear I heard something moving in the garden,' he says and you stare out into the dark, both of you listening, neither of you really wanting to hear anything.

'What sort of something?' you ask.

'How am I supposed to know?' he replies.

Then you hear the noise, like something pushing through the bushes.

'You hear that?' Joe whispers.

'Yeah.'

As your eyes adjust to the dark you start to make out a shape moving across the overgrown lawn. To begin with it looks like a grotesquely huge bird, hopping through the grass but then, as it moves out of the shade of one of the trees and into the moonlight, you see it's a man, wearing tracksuit bottoms and a hoodie.

'So there was someone here,' you say, 'that must have been whoever was inside.'

'Probably,' Joe says.

Suddenly the figure stops and looks towards you. Then, as if terrified by something, turns and runs back into the trees.

'Weird,' you say. 'What scared him off? You think he heard us?'

'Maybe,' Joe replies. 'You think we should follow him? Find out what scared him?'

NO WAY! GO TO 26.
YEAH, WHY NOT? GO TO 38.

6

You cut through the garden, using the putters as a way of beating back the more overgrown bushes. You head back past the circle of benches now buried in ivy. Beyond that, the gardens open out into an open section of overgrown lawn and, finally, the maze.

'I bet you can't get through it now,' you say. 'It'll have grown too much since the fire.'

Joe peers through the entrance. 'Actually, it's fine, a bit overgrown but we can still walk around it easily enough.'

But do you want to? That's the question. Joe certainly thinks so because he's hung his putter off one of the longer hedge branches and headed inside. He's all the way down one path and turning the corner into another.

With a sigh, you dump your putter and follow.

The hedges are a couple of metres high. Joe was right. Although it's overgrown, with lots of thin tendrils reaching out and brushing you as you pass, it's perfectly easy to walk along the path. Using the light on your camera you jog to catch up with Joe.

'Please tell me we're not going all the way in,' you ask him. 'I'd kind of like to see the hotel at some point tonight, not, y'know, spend hours getting lost in here.'

'Lost?' Joe replies. 'Who's going to get lost? It's not that big. We'll be fine. It's like that movie… what's it called?'

'*The Shining*?'

'Yeah, that's it.'

'The one where the psycho with the axe gets *really lost in a maze and dies*?' You couldn't give those last few words more weight if you were to turn them into a neon sign and hang them around his neck.

'Yeah. Good movie.'

'I'll remind you of that when we're found at the middle of this thing in a few months' time, frozen to death like he was.'

'How are you going to remind me? You'll be dead too.'

'Smart-arse.'

'Anyway, he was mental, not clever like us!' With that he pulls a funny face and starts leaping off through the maze, dancing around like a crazy man. 'Heeeere's Weller!' he shouts, pretending to be the guy from the movie.

'Joe!' you shout as he vanishes around the next bend. 'Mate!' You hear a mad laugh as he runs past you on the other side of the hedge. You roll your eyes, then sigh, 'Yeah, not mental at all.' And then you chase after him.

As you clear the next corner there's no sign of Joe so you keep running. You come to a junction and stop for a second, listening carefully. You hear a rustling from the left-hand fork so you run that way, you can see the light of his camera bobbing up and down in front of you, dancing across the hedge like a searchlight looking for an escaped prisoner.

'Joe!' you shout, 'stop pissing about!'

You turn another corner and catch a glimpse of him, just a flash of grey in the beam of your own light, running off to the right. 'Fine,' you say and keep running.

At the next junction there's no sign of him so you turn your light off, thinking his will give him away. You're bound to be able to see it, even through the hedges. But there's nothing, it's completely dark. Then you hear a low chuckle, someone trying to hide the fact they're laughing, coming from the other side of the hedge to your right. Fine, you think, two can play at that game. You start moving again but leave your camera light off. As your eyes adjust, there's enough light coming from the moon to see your way and now you're following the noises he's making. There's that laugh again, coming from your right this time. So you turn at the next right, look down the next path and – just for a second – see a dark shape moving off down to the left. You run to catch up, take the left path and then stop again, listening for your next clue as to where he is.

Is he whispering? Who's he think he's talking to? Talking into the camera probably, though that's kind of pointless because with the light off it's not like it's going to be able to see anything. The whispering is close by so you move slower, trying to be quiet. If he thinks he's going to leap out at you and make you jump you'll soon show him.

The whispering stops, so do you. Where is he? He must be close by. Then you hear the sound of someone moving fast behind the hedge to your right. You look around for the entrance to that path and chase after them. You're damned if he's going to catch you out with this, only one person's getting the scare of their life in here and it ain't gonna be you.

You lose him again for a moment but then the whispering is back and it sounds like it's just around the corner. So you walk very carefully, making sure you don't make a sound.

The whispering gets louder as you approach a bend in the path. There's a turn on your left and the whispering is definitely coming from just down there. The whispering stops just as you think you can make out some of the words. ('Sad, so, so sad.' What the hell was he talking about?) But you can still hear his breathing. You're surprised actually because Joe's fit and you wouldn't have thought he'd sound so out of breath having only run this short way. He really sounds like he's struggling though, his breath wheezing so much he almost sounds like an old man. There's a rustle of foliage and you can picture him, pressing himself against the hedge, waiting for you to come running along so he can jump out on you. Yeah… not tonight Joe, I'm right here and any minute now I'm going to run around that corner and I'm going to scream so loudly they'll hear me in the village. And you my friend, yes *you*, are going to absolutely wet yourself… You take a couple more steps and you reckon that if you were to shove your hand through the hedge you'd actually touch him, you're that close.

Which is when you hear Joe shout your name. But the voice isn't coming from just on the other side of the hedge. No. Joe's voice is coming from somewhere behind you, several rows away.

'Where the hell are you?' he shouts.

But… If that's Joe, then… *What the hell is on the other side of this hedge?!*

You'd followed it all the way here. Followed the sound it was making, the brief glimpses of it.

Joe shouts again and he's much closer now, heading towards you. You want to shout back but, even though the breathing sounds have stopped, whatever you followed must still be right there.

The light from Joe's camera hits you as he turns the corner and sees you.

'There you are!' he says 'What were you playing at? I saw you go running off and then you turned your light off and... what?' He's obviously seen the look on your face. 'What's the matter with you?'

'I was following you,' you reply, still not quite daring to raise your voice.

'No you weren't,' he says, 'you ran right past me at that first corner, I was only hiding in the hedge. But then you were running so fast, your light turned off, I lost track of you for a bit.'

He moves past you, turning down the path where whoever you were following – and it is *who*ever isn't it, Christ, please don't say it's *what*ever – should still be stood. But there's clearly nothing there. Because Joe just walks right past. 'I cheated,' he shouts, 'and climbed up one of the hedges. Way out's just here.'

You follow him, because... what else are you supposed to do? And he's right, one more turn and you're back out in the open air.

'I swear I was following something in there,' you say finally, 'I heard it. Whispering and stuff.'

'Probably just the wind,' he replies, 'rustling the hedges.' He reaches out and does just that and, yes, maybe that's what it was.

Maybe.

'Anyway,' he adds, 'that's enough messing about out here. Let's get inside shall we?'

GO TO 30.

You shove the door open and it swings back with a low creak. You turn on the lights. There's this weird feeling of stepping into someone's life just moments after they've left it. A bed, its covers thrown back. A couple of mugs, now thick with mould, on the desk. An old magazine about vintage cars splayed open on the floor.

You pick it up. 'Someone likes old rides.'

'You should introduce them to your mum,' says Joe.

You dump the magazine on the bed and step through into the bathroom. In the gloom of the bath something scuttles towards the plughole. A spider so large you wonder if it'll even manage to fold itself into the pipe.

The sill in front of a small, frosted glass window has become a cemetery for flies but some are still alive somewhere, their buzzing echoing in the small tiled room. The noise seems to be coming from

everywhere but as much as you look around you can't see them. You catch your reflection in the bathroom mirror and just for a second you don't recognise yourself. You look so pale, almost ill.

And the buzzing. The constant buzzing. But where are the flies that are making all this noise?

Behind you the bathroom door slams shut and the light goes out.

'Joe?' you shout, 'stop pissing about.'

The sound of flies gets even louder and you stumble towards the door, stroking the wall, trying to find the door handle or the light switch, you don't care which. You've found the fly at least, it's beating against your face as you try and get out. No, not just one fly, definitely more than that. Your face is being tickled all over. Feather-light touches on your skin. Like the tingle of static electricity. The buzzing is so loud, filling the room, filling your head. Are they in your hair? It feels like it, crawling all over your scalp, all over your face. How many flies are there for Christ's sake? You screw your eyes tightly closed as they crawl over your eyelids and you can imagine their little probosces stabbing out to drink your tears. You want to open your mouth to shout to Joe again, but if you do that they'll crawl inside won't they? They'll be running all over your teeth, all over your tongue, scampering down your throat, finding places in the warm darkness to lay their eggs. You pinch your nose closed with your fingers, but what about your ears? Can they crawl inside your ears? Into your sinuses? Into your *head*?

You beat your other hand against the wall. Where's the door? Where's the damned light switch? This is ridiculous! You're just panicking, your imagination getting out of control. There can't be this many flies in here, there just can't be. It feels like the entire room is full of them now. More flies than air. Ridiculous. As your palm skims the wall you can feel the their bodies popping under your stabbing fingers, spilling thick, sticky guts.

WHERE'S THE SWITCH? WHERE'S THE DOOR?

The sound is so loud now you can barely think. A hum that makes your bones shake. It feels like if it gets any louder it will actually break you. How can it be so loud?

Inside that hum is the sense of something moving. Something much larger than a fly. Something lifting itself up out of the bath perhaps. Something that is even now reaching out towards you. Something whose touch will feel like sharp bones. Sharp bones covered in tiny little hairs. Something with wings that could wrap you up and never let you go. Something that, when it buzzes, will shake you to pieces.

The light comes back on and there's nothing. Just that pile of dead flies on the window sill. You yank open the door and run back into the bedroom where Joe is looking through the drawers of the desk.

'What's wrong with you?' he asks.

You look into the empty bathroom and you just don't have the words. You were imagining it. Of course you were. You must have been. Mustn't you?

'Nothing,' you tell him. 'Just got shut in there with the light off that's all. Thanks for that.'

'I didn't touch it. I presumed you were having a cheeky piss.'

You decide you believe him, because that's easier. Because if he didn't slam the door shut something else did and you really don't want to go there.

'Let's get out of here,' you say, heading back towards the corridor outside the room.

GO TO 2.

'Let's just get in there,' you say, 'there's no point hanging around out here.'

'Fair enough.'

'Is it even going to be open?' you ask as you walk through the arch to the front door.

'Don't think that's going to be a problem, mate,' says Joe as he shines his camera light on the door.

Heavy, fire-stained wood, it's been split with one door hanging loose while the other tilts inwards, splintered and warped, like it lost a fight with a lump hammer.

While you hold his camera for him, Joe grabs the loose door and tries to push it inwards so there's space to get past.

'Pretty good!' he grunts with sarcasm, because it's still attached by one huge rusted hinge that seems determined to stop people getting in.

Joe's pushing and pulling. At last he manages to get it moving and there's a crack of splintered wood that sounds like a gunshot as the hinge finally pops free.

All in all, this isn't your most subtle entrance to an abandoned building.

'You think anyone heard that?' you ask.

'Nobody about for miles.' He's got a point. In the car the village was a good ten minutes away. Why anyone would have wanted to stay the night here, so far from everybody and everything, you have no idea.

'Hello?' Joe calls, his voice, even though it's quiet, echoing back from the hallway beyond.

'This is sketchy, mate,' you tell him.

"THIS IS THE DOCTOR OF SEXUALLY ACTIVE YOUNG BOYS SPEAKING, HOW MAY I HELP YOU TODAY?"

'Yeah,' he agrees, then grins, 'classic abandoned building.'

You step inside and the smell of the hotel punches you hard.

'Jesus,' says Joe, 'it's been like, a year, but this place still reeks of the fire.'

You sweep the light from your camera around the entrance hall. It's a huge room. Big staircase leading up from the middle, to the right of that an old-fashioned lift, a concertinaed gate in front of a heavy wooden door. To the left, a choice of two corridors leading further into the building. Straight ahead, there's a reception desk built from dark oak. On the wall right next to you, a soot-stained picture of an old man in a white wig leers down at you as if he's offended by the fact that you've just walked into his house. Maybe he is.

On the other side there's a large mirror, the dirty, warped glass reflecting the light back at you.

Somewhere, the sound echoing around the room, a phone begins to ring making you both jump.

'Seriously?' you ask.

'Oi nah,' says Joe with a grin. He starts looking around for the phone. 'Where's it coming from? Can you tell?'

'Somewhere over there I think,' you say, pointing past the stairs.

He sees it on a side-table and grabs it, answering it in the classic silly-Weller-voice, 'This is the Doctor of Sexually Active Young Boys speaking, how may I help you today?' There's a moment of silence. 'How dare you ignore the words of the Prince of all Gorgeous…'

'What on earth are you doing?' you interrupt him.

'The little rats aren't responding!'

'How's the phone even still working?' you ask.

He shrugs. 'Obviously never cut the line, mate. Very weird…' He hangs up. 'I wonder if there's any power?' he says. 'Wouldn't need it for an old phone like this, but it's worth a look.'

You both move over to the wall where there's a bank of light switches. Joe flicks them all down and some of the lights come on. Not all the bulbs still work but enough that you can see the room clearly now.

He pours out a decent measure for the two of you and then shoves the bottle back on the shelf. 'The builders can have the rest.'

You take your drinks and sit down at one of the tables.

'So much for no more pissing about,' you say, taking a sip of your warm vodka.

'This isn't pissing about,' Joe replies, 'it's preparation. So… more about some of the stuff that happened here. What shall we talk about?'

'Go back to the beginning,' you suggest, 'the priory that was here. What was that all about?'

'Well,' says Joe, 'I don't know much about it to be honest because I could only find a couple of brief mentions of it online. Basically though, it was a group of monks who set themselves up here. The locals didn't like them much, which one of the pieces I read suggested was because the monks weren't Christian, you know, they were worshipping something else…'

'Black magic and stuff?' you ask.

'Yeah, might not be true though.' He grins. 'Makes a better story though! So let's go with it. A bunch of monks lived here, worshipping the Devil. The locals were terrified of them and then one day…' he makes the sound of a something bursting into flames.

'You think the locals did it?'

'Either that or the monks kept trying to talk to something in Hell and finally… it turned up!' He finishes his drink. 'After that, the place was burned out, a ruin, but the locals still avoided the site because they said this bit of land was cursed, that even with the monks gone something lived on out here. Then, hundreds of years later…'

'Isaac Godling goes and builds a house on it.'

'Yep.'

'What do you think?' you ask. 'Can a bit of land actually be cursed?'

'Let's keep looking and see if we can find out.'

GO TO 49.

'It's so good to get out of that place for a few minutes,' Toby Hurrell thinks, sneaking past the stupid crazy golf and over to the pond.

He quickly checks to see if there are any guests around – assistant managers really shouldn't be sneaking a crafty smoke in the grounds. Happy that he has the place to himself, he lights up and leans on one of the decorative statues. It's an ugly-looking water maiden with a snide look on her face. If she could speak you'd swear the first thing she'd do is moan about the water bucket she's carrying, then add that she had no choice but to carry it because everyone else around here was an idiot.

Which reminds him of his boss. Ms Grace is a nightmare. She's always been a nightmare. When Toby first joined the staff here it was replacing someone who had finally had enough of her manager's attitude and stormed out to find a better job – by which she meant *any* job – unable to bear another moment dealing with Ms Grace. The rest of the staff had given him a look when he turned up, all smiling and full of determination and enthusiasm. 'You'll learn,' that look said. 'You haven't got a chance mate.'

Now, six months later, Ms Grace is worse than ever. The previous assistant manager had been here for two years. Toby was fairly sure that after that amount of time he wouldn't have been able to just leave, he'd have had to kill his boss instead, then sit down in the dining room to throw food at the guests while waiting for the police to arrive.

'Just ignore her,' he thought, 'that's what you have to do, just ignore her, otherwise you're going to go mad and no job is worth that.'

Wind strolled lazily through the garden and sent a swirl of dead leaves into the pond. He should probably fish them out but he couldn't

11

There's no way you're getting in the lift and you tell Joe so.

'Fair enough,' he replies.

So you both put on a pair of pink dresses and dance around in front of the cameras like the absolute pussies you are.

TURN TO 3 AND GROW A PAIR. YOU HAVE NO CHOICE, GET IN THE DAMN LIFT.

You open the door and step inside the office. There's paperwork spread everywhere. A filing cabinet is open and chunks of old letters, bills and invoices have been grabbed and thrown around the place. Above a desk is a bank of TV monitors. The security cameras, you think, this is where the manager would keep an eye on the place.

'So!' Joe, looks into the camera. 'The last manager of the hotel was a woman called Paulette Grace and apparently she was…' he pulls a face, 'well, a bit of a dodgy specimin to say the least. It's hard to tell about these things because, you know, so many stories end up getting told and ninety per cent of it is probably bollocks. But apparently she started off OK in the job but then, after a few years, she started to go a bit strange. After the fire lots of members of staff talked about it. Apparently she really got into the history of this place from before it was a hotel.'

'When the Godlings lived here?'

'Yeah. She actually moved in to the hotel, I mean… they had spare rooms so it wasn't a big deal but… She never wanted to leave the place. And when she was working, she'd spend hours shut in here refusing to come out, just reading about Isaac and the Godling family. If staff complained they just got their shifts messed with so, you know, in the end they just got on with it.'

You look around the room and, amongst all the mess you start to see a pattern forming. In amongst the discarded invoices, old menus and advertising copy are sheets of A4 paper with a handwritten scrawl on them. You pull a couple out. 'Don't deserve it here,' says one. 'He hates them all,' says another.

'What the hell do these mean?' you wonder.

Grinning, Joe holds one up. 'HE'S INSIDE ME!' it says. He raises an eyebrow.

There are old photographs too, some clipped from newspapers, others from books. The same old man. Neat, oiled hair, dull, smart clothes, eyes that look like there's no life in them at all. He's painfully thin, with a nose so huge you could pick him up and chop firewood with it.

'Isaac Godling,' explains Joe. 'Told you she was obsessed.'

NO KIDDING, GO TO 41 AND THEN COME BACK HERE.

'Mental,' you say. 'What is it with this place? Did nobody decent live here?'

'If they did they didn't last long,' he replies. 'It's just…' he shakes his head, 'it's a bad place. Do you believe that? Like, that a place can actually be broken?'

'Maybe,' you admit. 'I don't know… but you go some places and there's just an atmosphere. They don't feel comfortable.'

'Yeah, and this place is one of them.' He suddenly grins, 'So shall we keep having a look around it then or what?'

GO TO 34.

The door opened and the maid entered. Jessica, Jennifer, whoever she was.

'What's your name again?' Clarissa asked, as the maid quietly went about the business of collecting her dirty chamber pot.

'Emily, madam.'

'Oh.' She hadn't even got that right. Or was this a new maid? Or a vision? No. Surely visions didn't concern themselves with chamber pots. 'I do seem to keep forgetting. I apologise.'

'Please don't worry yourself, madam.' Emily said, leaving with the chamber pot and closing the door behind her.

'She seems pleasant,' said her son.

'Does she? If she was really pleasant she'd let me leave this room, don't you think?'

'She thinks you're mad.'

'So I am, no excuse to let me live like this.'

The door opened again and Emily returned with a fresh chamber pot and a small silver tray with a bowl on it.

'What's for lunch today?' Clarissa asked. She could see for herself but she liked to talk to the people who came in here, she may be a prisoner but at least she wasn't forced to be a silent one.

'Beef broth madam.'

'The same as yesterday.'

'The doctor says it will help build up your strength.'

Clarissa rolled her eyes. What was the point in building up her strength? It didn't take much effort to sit here, day after day.

'I wouldn't know about that, madam,' the maid said, surprising Clarissa. Had she spoken out loud? She had been sure she'd only *thought* about the absurdity of it all. The last thing she intended to do was give the maid the idea she might be angry. Maids didn't like to talk to angry people and Clarissa did so want to talk to… to… Emma was it?

'Emily, mother,' her son reminded her.

'Quite so,' Clarissa agreed.

The maid advanced with the bowl of broth and a spoon.

'Emily?' Clarissa asked, pleased to have got the name right.

'Please madam,' Emily said, already aware of what her mistress was going to say, 'don't ask if you can hold the bowl and spoon yourself. You know I'm not allowed to do that.'

'I'm perfectly capable,' Clarissa insisted.

'I don't doubt it madam, but I have my orders and it's been made very clear what will happen to me should I not obey them.'

'Yes, wouldn't want to have to share this room would you?'

She opened her mouth to receive the first serving of beef broth. It steamed on the soup spoon, far too hot to swallow, surely? This wasn't unusual. The maid never liked to linger here and was always terribly concerned with getting this business over and done with as quickly as possible.

Then the maid threw the whole bowl of hot broth into Clarissa's face. Clarissa screamed, the liquid dripping off her reddening face. Even though she knew her hands were securely fastened, she couldn't help thrashing involuntarily, desperate to wipe the remains of the food off her cheeks.

'Why… why?' she sobbed.

'Why not?' said Isaac. There was no longer any sign of the maid. Had she dreamed her completely or had she blacked out? That did happen sometimes, whole chunks of the day vanishing, day becoming night becoming day again. She didn't mind that, anything to make the tedium pass quicker. 'Lick your lips if you're hungry.'

Clarissa shuddered, trying not to sob. She hated it when she sobbed. There was little opportunity for her to retain her dignity here as it was, crying just made her feel even more of a failure.

'Everyone cries sometimes,' her son said, 'I did, when I died, thick and hot. I couldn't tell what was blood and what was tears.'

'It's common enough with regressive types like this,' explained Dr Turnbull, 'they no longer know how to express their emotions properly. They may cry at a vague sound or smile at the death of a pet. It all becomes terribly confused.'

Terribly confused. Was her husband still here? Was she? She could feel the cool breeze on her face – a welcome relief after the scalding from the broth – and somewhere she could hear a train pulling out of the station. Ah yes, there it was, the train taking her eldest son away to the War.

'I'd do it all again,' her son said, stood behind her on the platform. 'One has to do one's duty after all.'

And then she was back in the room again. And alone.

The door opened and the maid walked in.

'Hello madam,' she said, 'Broth again for lunch I'm afraid.'

GO TO 33.

W hich is when the lower stair, the stair you thought was safe, starts to move. There's a loud creak and you shout in panic as Joe pulls you as hard as he can. Your left foot kicks out at the steps that are now caving in, wood splitting, carpet tearing. You want to look down, to see what's happening, but you keep your eyes fixed on Joe as he leans back and tugs you to safety.

The pair of you scrabble a little, not wanting to both be on the same stair in case your combined weight is enough to break it. You keep moving up the last few stairs, just desperate to be clear. Once you get to the landing you stop and look down.

'Well, that's made things complicated,' says Joe, looking at the huge gap in the stairs that's now opened up.

'Yeah,' you agree. 'There's no way I'm jumping that gap, the minute either of us lands on the other side the stairs will just give way. They were strong enough to step carefully on but a heavy landing?'

'There should be some backstairs or something,' says Joe. 'Or the lift. If the power's working we can probably use that.'

Which sounds even more terrifying than jumping the stairs in your opinion but you let it go.

You turn to look across the landing and that's when you see the problem's bigger than you thought. The damage here is immense, a big section of the floor has sunk down, clearly unsafe. Walls are thick with soot, doors half burned away, the place is a mess.

'You said the fire started here?' you ask Joe.

'Yeah,' he says, 'though I didn't know it was this bad.'

GO TO SECTION 41 AND THEN RETURN HERE.

'There's no way we should cross that way.' You point at the area where the fire obviously started. 'It's amazing it hasn't caved in already but I bet it will the minute we try and walk on it.'

Joe nods. 'Old buildings were made to last I guess, heavy wood, well built. It burned up but didn't fall down. You're right though, we ain't walking on it.' He looks up. 'And look at the stairs that way. Heat rises.'

You look up and, sure enough, you can see a big section of the stairs leading up to the second floor has now burned away completely. So, you can't go down, you can't go up. If there's a set of stairs at the back of the building you'd have to cross the damaged section to get to them and that's not happening. Joe's right, you're basically trapped on this floor, restricted to the few rooms at the front of the building or… you'll have to take the lift.

'So what do you want to do?' he asks. 'Look around on this floor or try the lift?'

FINE, LET'S TRY THE LIFT, WHAT CHOICE DO WE HAVE? GO TO 50.

NO, SORRY BUT NO. LET'S LOOK AROUND AND SEE IF THERE'S ANOTHER WAY. GO TO 45.

She's wearing a fussy old dress, and is giving you both the sort of sideways look that says: 'That thing you're doing. Stop it. Stop it now.'

'Who's this?' you ask.

'No idea,' admits Joe, 'nothing to do with this place I don't think, just a picture. Isaac probably bought it for decoration.'

'Some decoration. Why would you hang her on the wall?' you wonder. 'She's clearly not enjoying it.'

'Maybe she was someone famous,' says Joe.

'Winner of the Most Angry Woman Competition 1765?'

'Frowniest Painted Troll.'

Further along the corridor, facing each other, there are two rooms with doors ajar.

'Which one?' Joe asks.

'Does it matter?' you reply.

I don't know, does it?

LEFT? GO TO 25
RIGHT? GO TO 7

her worse if anything. Isaac didn't care, by then he was shagging his secretary, Genevieve. He married her in the end.'

'How long did *she* last before he locked her up?'

'She died on the stairs,' Joe says, 'a few years later. Fell down them.'

You look back up at the picture and your eyes are drawn to the wall behind it. Further up, water seems to be trickling down from where it meets the ceiling.

'Where's that coming from?' you wonder. 'Something's leaking somewhere on the fourth floor.'

Joe looks up. 'I think the tower's directly above here. Maybe one of the pipes has burst or something.'

The water is running faster now, streaming down the wall in a shiny sheet. It froths slightly and you reach out and touch it. 'It's kind of slimy.' You sniff your fingers. 'And smells of perfume or something.'

Joe touches a particularly frothy patch and smells it. 'Yeah… bubble bath or something. Weird.'

The water starts to darken and now it looks pink. It's because of the old pipes isn't it? That's what it is. Old copper pipes. You say as much.

'Maybe,' Joe says hesitantly before trying to sound more positive. 'Yeah, must be.'

Because the last thing you want to think is that it might be blood.

GO TO 40.

"I THINK THE TOWER'S DIRECTLY ABOVE HERE."

'Skinny-dipping in the pond!' he shouts.

You keep hold of the putters, using them to help you beat your way through the sections where the bushes have started to block the path. In a few minutes you're on a large terrace, wooden benches surrounding the large pond. In the corners, four statues look down over the murky water. From the way a cherub is holding itself you figure it used to piss in there. The water's so filthy you don't think anybody would complain if it still did.

'There's no way I'm going in that,' Joe announces, 'smells almost as dodgy as Calfreezy's trainers!'

You peer down into the water, completely black in the moonlight, leaves forming islands of scum on its surface.

'Yeah,' you agree, 'it'll be bloody freezing as well.'

Joe sits on one of the benches and you film him as he drops into the character of a posh hotel guest.

'Jolly lovely,' he says, 'though I can't seem to get a tan going.' His face grows serious. 'Shouldn't joke really, not after what happened in there.'

'What?' you ask.

'It was on the day of the fire…' he says.

GO TO 10.

Leaving the games room, you spot a door at the end of the corner with a big sign on it saying 'Emergency Exit'. 'Backstairs maybe?' you wonder.

'Got to be hasn't it?' Joe agrees, moving to the door and pulling it open.

On the other side, beyond a deep red carpet, there's none of the posh decoration, just old plastered walls and a stairway climbing up through the floors.

'No lights here,' says Joe, 'not that I can see anyway.'

'Should be fine,' you reply, keeping your light pointing at the stairs.

'This was probably the servants' stairs,' says Joe as you start to climb up. 'You know, like on *Downton Abbey*.'

'You watched *Downton Abbey*?'

'Well,' he admits, 'sometimes it's sort of been on while I was in the same room. Not on purpose. Not because I wanted to watch it…'

'You love it,' you joke, 'it's your favourite show.'

'Sometimes I dress up,' he says, playing along. 'I put on one of those long dresses and eat tiny little triangle sandwiches.' He looks at you with the most serious, sad-looking face he can imagine. 'It's the only time I'm really able to be myself.'

'Yeah…' you roll your eyes. You've reached the first floor. 'Keep going?' you ask.

'Yeah, let's do it, it's probably in a very raucous condition, that's where the fire started.'

You keep climbing, coming to a window on your right. There's no sign of fire damage here and, with the lack of light, you can see through it clearly enough. You look out on the garden, the moon shining back at you from a big rectangle of water that must be a pond

or swimming pool. Over to the left, the big black cube of the maze. Just for a second, you're convinced you see movement out there. A couple of shapes making their way along the path that leads to the pool.

'I think there's somebody out there,' you say.

Joe peers through the window but, whoever it was, they're gone now (if they were ever there). 'Can't see anything.'

'Probably nothing,' you reply, half believing it.

You carry on climbing until you get to the third floor.

'Shall we have a look what's here?' Joe asks. 'Or go right to the top?

EXPLORE THE THIRD FLOOR? GO TO 57.
KEEP GOING? GO TO 32.

'He murdered a girl?' you ask.

'Maybe a few girls,' Joe answers, 'we just don't know. A couple of true-crime blogs talk about it. There were some people who went missing from around here after the Second World War. There was never any proof, just local gossip really. He'd been seen with some of the girls, y'know? And had a reputation as a bit of a player. Someone said they saw him driving away from where one of the bodies was found. Someone else reckoned they saw bloodstains on the front of his car. But by the time the bodies were found, Thom Godling was always abroad. It was nothing you could pin a case on, the police never even arrested him.'

'A serial killer? You think his dad covered it up?'

'Maybe. It's the sort of thing he probably would have done.'

You move away from the portrait but you can't help thinking about how broken this family was. Cruel Isaac. The wife he locked away. The son that might have been a murderer. It was just…

There's an almighty crashing sound which seems to be coming from towards the front of the hotel.

'What the hell was that?' you ask, the two of you running towards the source of the noise.

You step back into the reception area of the hotel and the air is filled with dust and soot. Looking towards the stairs you see that they've caved in, the whole central section of the first staircase now nothing but a ragged hole of torn carpet and splintered wood.

'Jesus!' Joe stares at the damage. 'We could have been trying to climb up that when it fell in.'

'Yeah.' You imagine what could have happened if you'd been walking up them. Maybe you would have been OK, maybe you could have jumped to safety, but you look at the jagged splints of wood jutting up from the hole and you can't help imagining yourself pierced by one, sliding slowly down it like something raw speared on a meat skewer.

'Well,' says Joe, 'we weren't so there's no point in panicking about it. Shows we have to be careful though.'

'Damn right we do,' you agree, 'looks like we won't be exploring upstairs then.' You glance at the lift. 'Because there's no way I'm risking that thing,' you add, pointing towards it. 'We might be OK,' he says, 'I bet there's a back staircase as well, let's have a look.'

Just as you start to move back towards the corridor the phone starts ringing again.

Joe grabs it, seeming almost angry at the interruption.

'Look,' he shouts into the phone, 'there's nobody here OK?' Then his face falls.

'What?' you ask.

He beckons you over and tilts the phone away from his ear so you can both hear. The voice on the other end is faint, a dry, cracking whisper, that sounds like it's on the verge of tears.

'Katy?' the man asks. 'Katy, if you can hear me... I'm sorry, OK? So... so sorry... I don't know what came over me. I really don't.'

Joe pulls a questioning face at you. 'WTF?' You shrug. Then the voice changes, suddenly become angry.

'You shouldn't be there!' it screams, 'You shouldn't know!' and then whoever it is hangs up.

'What the hell was that all about?' you ask.

'No clue, mate,' Joe replies, replacing the handset. He pauses then lifts it again and presses a button on the phone.

'What are you doing?' you ask.

'Calling him back,' he grins.

'Why?!!' you ask.

'Why not?' Joe waits for a second. The phone is answered.

'Katy?' asks the quiet voice on the other end.

'She's still pissed off with you,' says Joe. 'So, you know, don't call back.' He hangs up.

'Evil,' you say, laughing.

'Yeah, well, he shouldn't have shagged around should he?'

'How do you know he did?'

'Come on mate, bloke ringing up some girl begging for forgiveness? *Of course* he shagged around. Come on, let's see if we can find the backstairs.'

The phone starts ringing again. 'Just leave it,' you say.

'I probably should,' Joe agrees. But he doesn't. 'Yes?' he answers in a silly voice.

'I see you,' says the voice, 'I've been watching you. I like to watch.'

'Well that sounds like you're a bloody paedo…' says Joe.

'Mind melted,' the voice says, then laughs. 'I'll kill the pair of you soon.' Then hangs up.

'"Mind melted"?' asks Joe, 'What sort of weird insult is that? Balls to him.'

He puts the phone down and you head back along the corridor.

GO TO 39.

'I'm thinking,' you say, 'that a manager's office is probably the most boring room in the place. What are we going to find? The haunted hole punch?'

'Alright then, we'll keep going.'

The corridor leads to a pair of double doors marked 'Private'. Off to your right, the corridor continues but, let's be honest, nothing makes you want to look somewhere more than being told you shouldn't.

Joe pushes the doors open and the hinges squeal like terrified pigs. The double doors were obviously fire doors because, other than a few damp stains from the water that's dripped through the floors above, there's really no fire damage on this side.

Walking down the corridor there are a few small staff rooms on either side, one with lockers and a table and a couple of easy chairs.

'Probably where they spent their breaks,' you say, picking up an old magazine and flicking through it. 'Oh my God!' you shout sarcastically, 'Sophie and Katie hooked up on *Love Island*!'

'Ah…' Joe looks wistful, 'important moments from history.'

One of the lockers is open and Joe's face lights up as he pulls out a chef's uniform. You wonder how many seconds it'll take for him to decide he wants to put it on. Just as you finish wondering that and put the magazine back down on the table, you turn round and see that he's already wearing it.

'What do you think?' he says.

'I think I don't want you cooking anything for me.'

'I've got the kitchen skills to pay the bills, mate,' he replies.

You head out of the room and further down the corridor where another pair of doors lead to the kitchen. You try the lights but they don't work so you make do with what you have.

'Here we go!' he announces, 'I'm home.'

You're already setting up the camera as he starts going through all the cupboards.

'There's actually still stuff here,' he says. 'Tins and packets.' He holds up a tin of tomato soup. 'Cheeky bastards! I bet they threw a few leaves on the top of this and charged a fortune for it.'

In another cupboard he finds some saucepans, in a drawer some knives and cooking utensils. He starts dragging things out and then looks directly to camera.

'Greetings and welcome to *Haunted & Abandoned Cooking with Weller*. Tonight I will be making that classic dish: dustbins on bread with a dodgy bean surprise.'

'Sounds nice,' you say.

'It derives from the streets of Grimsby town.'

He grabs a pan and opens the can of tomato soup.

'First you take some tomato soup,' he upturns it into the pan and starts whisking, 'then grab some…' he checks the next can as he peels off the lid, 'kidney beans and whack those naughty little boys in there as well.' He grabs a packet at random, tears it open and dumps the contents into the mix. 'Followed by…' he checks, 'shit the bed… erm… ant pellets, you know, for that really gorgeous touch.'

'I am not eating that,' you tell him, 'just in case you wondered about that. Don't. Really don't. Because it's not happening.'

'Ant pellets have mulitple benefits for the skull and mind, you see,' he continues.

'Unless you're an ant,' you mutter.

'Next you take…' He grabs another packet and tears it open. The air is now full of flour. 'some flour and…' he coughs, clouds of the stuff still raining down all over him, 'just, you know, let that spread around the room a bit. Just to take the edge off.'

Another tin.

'Finally, you throw in some…' tinned peaches slop out of the tin and into the pan, sounding exactly like anyone who might eat this meal would a few minutes after finishing it, 'I… you know, I seriously can't see cos of all that flour shit. What was that?'

'Peaches I think.'

'Peaches. Fine. So yeah! Add some delicious peaches and then…' He's beating the hell out of the food in the saucepan, really thrashing it, treating it as if it had just said something horrible about his mum, 'mix the concoction together.'

You step back a little because, honestly, Joe's spreading a good deal of that slop all over the place. He puts the pan down.

'Now all you need to do is heat it up.' He puts the pan on the hob and reaches for the dial, 'Boil it to death for about five hours and then…'

There's a loud bang and a bright flash of light.

'Jesus!' Joe hurls himself back out of the way but whatever caused the brief explosion, all is quiet now.

'What the hell was that?' you ask.

'Mate, I have literally no idea. I didn't even think the gas for the hob would still be connected.'

The lights come on, just for a second, then cut out again.

'Yeah,' you say, 'about that.'

'OK.' Joe pulls off the chef's uniform, uses it to wipe a couple of splashes from his face then flings it to the floor. 'No more pissing about. Let's keep exploring.'

You move back out into the corridor, and head to the next door on your left. 'The Isaac Godling Room' says a plaque next to the door.

'Let's take a look,' says Joe.

You open the door and step inside.

"TONIGHT I WILL BE MAKING THAT CLASSIC DISH: DUSTBINS ON BREAD WITH DODGY BEAN SURPRISE."

GO TO 55.

properly. You can't just quit and walk away in the middle of a conversation.'

'Conversation?' you reply, 'That wasn't a conversation — that was being screamed at!'

He rubs at his face, half thrilled half terrified. 'I know, but… we have to.'

You get up from the chair and walk away from the table. 'Seriously, that freaked me the fuck out! You can't want to do that again.'

He gets up and fetches the glass. 'Just a little more. We can ask them…' he pauses, thinking, 'because it was *them* wasn't it? That wasn't just one spirit. Maybe that's why it was so intense. That was a crowd.'

'There's a crowd of the dead screaming at us and you want to keep talking?' You can't even believe he's being serious about this.

'That's what this has always been about,' he says, 'all of these buildings, all of these videos. We wanted to find proof. Now something like this happens and you want to just run away from it?'

'It's dangerous!'

'It's a glass on a board,' he replies, 'how dangerous can that be?'

'We're talking to the dead!'

'And we haven't finished it properly,' he replies, 'if you want to talk about dangerous, all the books say that you have to close the conversation.'

You can't believe this. So it's dangerous to stop but terrifying to continue. You seriously wish you'd never started this. Maybe never come to the place at all for that matter.

He sits back down, putting the glass in place. He stares at you, 'Please. I can't do it on my own. Just a couple of minutes more?'

You sigh. This is ridiculous. But what if he's right? What if it's more dangerous to stop?

DO YOU PUT YOUR FINGERS BACK ON THE GLASS? GO TO 44.
DO YOU WALK AWAY? GO TO 61.

You head down to the ground floor, Joe continuing to tell Mooney all about the night's events.

You step out from the stairs into the corridor that leads back towards reception.

'We've even had some guy ringing up,' Joe says as we pass the phone, 'screaming down the line at us.' He grabs the handset from the cradle. 'Hang about…'

'Probably just a wrong number,' says Mooney who is looking at one of the suits of armour displayed against the wall, but now seems worried, 'You shouldn't really be using the phone, the bank will see the records.'

'It's only a quick one,' explains Joe, hitting the button to return the last call. He looks at you. 'You're filming, yeah?'

You know that someone is about to get pranked, and you're right, absolutely right, you just don't know who.

'It's ringing,' says Joe.

And that's when the phone in Mooney's pocket starts to buzz.

For a minute, you, Joe and Mooney just stare at one another. Then Mooney smirks, pulls the phone out of his pocket and sends the call to voicemail.

'Alright,' he says, 'you got me. I admit it, OK, I was pranking you. I didn't think you'd mind. I thought it might just add something fun to the video.'

He sounds convincing enough and you can see Joe is ready to go with it. 'Seriously?' Joe says, 'that was you?'

Mooney's grinning, wandering back to the suit of armour. 'Just look at this thing,' he says. 'Amazing.'

'Yeah,' agrees Joe, 'there's a few of them around the house. Are you going to be selling them off?'

'Probably.' Mooney picks up the pikestaff the suit of armour is holding. It's a long pole with a shiny metal blade at one end. At the base of the blade a sharp hook curves out, just one more way to bleed. 'Look at this thing,' he says, 'those medieval bastards didn't believe in skimping when it came to stabbing you I guess.'

Something is niggling at you. 'Mind melted.'

'What?' asks Joe.

'On the phone, when you called, that's what you said,' you tell Mooney, 'Mind melted.'

'Did I?' asks Mooney.

'Yeah, and you'd said you'd been watching.'

'Yeah,' agrees Joe, 'you did.'

'Watching us in the dining room maybe?' you suggest. 'Give me your camera,' you say to Joe.

'Why?' he asks.

'Just do it would you?'

He pulls a face but hands it to you. You stop filming and scroll through the footage you've already got, finding the stuff of you and Joe in the dining room. You turn the camera and play it to them.

'Boys and girls, you are about to see an act of skill that will melt your minds!' you hear Joe say as he reaches to grab the tablecloth and try to pull it from the table without disturbing the cutlery. 'On the count of three! One… two… three!'

There's the sound of cutlery flying everywhere and then…

'Mind. Melted,' you say in the footage, your voice deadpan.

You stop the playback and hand the camera to Joe. He glances up at the ceiling, at the security camera that sits in a junction between this corridor and the next.

'On the cameras?' he wonders. 'But that would mean…'

'I've been here all night,' Mooney agrees. Grabbing the pikestaff and swinging it in a huge arc. It collides with the side of Joe's head and he falls to the floor.

'Jesus!' you shout, 'Mooney, what are you playing at?'

'Mooney's just my screen name,' he says 'you can call me Julian if you like.'

You have no idea what to do. Joe's on the ground, moaning low, a trail of blood running from a cut in the side of his head. He's lucky that the blade of the pikestaff hit him side on but he's still obviously hurt. And you're going to be next, because Moo… no, *Julian* is walking towards you, the blade of the pikestaff held low, pointing towards you.

There's no way you can get to Joe. Trying to fight Julian when he's pointing that thing at you is just a really good way of getting stabbed. You need to run. It's your only option. If he comes after you then Joe's safe. If you can keep ahead of him – or maybe even double back on him somehow – then you'll be safe too.

Yes. You really haven't got any other option.

So you run. As fast and hard as you can.

GO TO 35.

She had stopped listening, looking around the room, distracted by all there was to see. In the tower there was nothing but her bed and a chamberpot and there was a limit to how much either could entertain.

'It is said,' her husband continued, 'that once one has entered into a state of true lawlessness, true amorality, the whole world can open before you. All potentials can be achieved.'

He was getting quite excited now. Not his natural state by any means, but the herbal concoction he had consumed twenty minutes earlier was finally taking effect and his perceptions were becoming quite delusional. The books seemed to be singing. The candles dotted around the room were positively volcanic.

'And so,' he finished, 'you will excuse the discomfort of the next hour or so.' He opened the case of surgical tools he had purchased. 'But rest assured your pain is for the good of my further education.'

Clarissa ceased to be distracted by the sights of the room once the pain of her husband's experiments truly set in. Isaac, however, seemed blind to her suffering and deaf to her screams. He considered himself to be elsewhere.

Isaac believed he was seeing through the years themselves, he imagined himself a tiny spirit, scurrying around the room, watching as it aged and changed. He watched as his home became a place filled with countless strangers. 'Where are all these people from?' he wondered. 'What are they doing in my house? How dare they intrude here?'

He roamed the corridors and recoiled at the flames that sprung from the landing on the first floor, staring down from the painted eyes of his own portrait at a wailing madwoman who burned like a candle.

He watched the young intruders as they treated his home as if it were their own, trampling through his broken belongings. He reached out, desperate to crush them for trespassing here.

Finally, cold and desperate, the drugs fading in his system, he sat back in one of the armchairs, right here in the library, and felt the flesh finally waste away from his evil bones. He looked down on his own figure and saw himself for what he was, a terrible, worthless man. What had it all been for? Just misery and dust. If only he could remember this when he returned to himself. He could beg his wife to forgive him. He could lead a better life. He could be happy.

If only he could remember.

He fell to dust and what memory there was of his visions were dismissed as feverish nightmares, brought on by the ceaseless sound of his wife's screams.

GO TO 36.

"LET THE HAUNTED GOLFING CHAMPIONSHIPS COMMENCE."

You go next and, after what seems like a good effort – 'You see where it went?' 'I didn't hear it land.' – you both realise the ball is still right there in front of you and all you managed to hurl towards the model hotel was a clump of weeds. You take another swing and the stone angel has cause to regret your poor aim.

You keep taking it in turns, both of you getting close every now and then as you start to get the hang of your aim and the strength of swing needed. A few of your balls are now bouncing off the windows of the model hotel, one even skims across its roof before rebounding off the small version of the tower and ending up in the grass.

Finally, it's Joe that manages it, his ball looks as though it's going to fall short, bouncing on the lip of the roof but then it hops a little further and comes to rest at the foot of the tower.

'Yes!' he shouts, holding the club above his head like a champion. 'Weller with the golfing strike of dreams!'

In celebration he takes a swing at one more ball that sails off into the dark towards the actual hotel before – CRASH – hitting one of the windows.

'Oh shit!' he says.

'I wouldn't worry,' you tell him, 'it's all coming down in a week or so.'

'True. So you want to look out here a bit more? Go and check out the pond? Or maybe even the maze?'

HEAD TO THE POND? GO TO 17.
HEAD TO THE MAZE? GO TO 6.

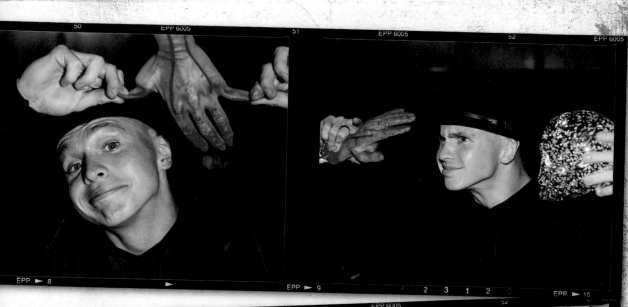

"THIS GEEZA LIKED HIS
MEAL SO MUCH HE LEFT
A WELL DODGY TIP."

'Mind. Melted,' you say, deadpan.

'Try it yourself then smart-arse.'

'Alright then,' you move to another table. You grab the edge of the tablecloth, turn to the camera and give it your best grin.

'Here we go!' shouts Joe, 'The youngster showing Weller how it's done! On three. One… two…' he leaves a long pause, because of course he does, 'three!'

There is now even more cutlery on the floor, you've also managed to step back and fall over a chair. So, yeah, all going well.

'OK,' you say, 'so it's harder than it looks.'

'Yeah,' Joe agrees. 'I guess the world tablecloth championships aren't for us.'

'Should we go into the history of the place a bit?' you suggest. 'You know, for the camera?'

'Yeah maybe,' says Joe, 'though there's so much of it it's hard to know where to start. In the beginning Priory Grange was an actual priory. A group of monks lived here and the locals were…' he thinks, 'scared of them I guess. They were probably a bunch of pussies if you ask me… one v. one in the ring and I'd have 'em all… Anyway, that burned down.'

'It burned down?' You didn't know this. 'So this place has been on fire twice?'

'Yeah, the first time was more successful. Back then, a building caught light and you'd all just be sitting round toasting boar's heads on it or something. It's not like they had the fire engines, or hoses even, and there's only so much you can do with a bucket you've had to carry for half an hour from the closest well. So, yeah, the first building – the actual priory – was gone. Locals, still being scared even though the monks were now up in smoke, avoided the place saying this patch of land was haunted. It's not until nearly five hundred years later, at the beginning of the twentieth century, that the land is bought by a guy called Isaac Godling. He builds this big house on it when he gets married because he's rich from selling loads of guns and munitions.'

'Gunrunner, nice.' You roll your eyes.

'It was all legal. He was in the Army, stationed in India during the 1890s – probably nicking loads of diamonds and stuff, like they did – and by the age of thirty, Isaac's minted, now flogging armaments to foreign countries and building this place.'

'What was he like?' you ask.

'He was the worst. His first wife, Clarissa went mad after the Second World War.'

'Why, was she in it?'

'Both her sons went over to fight. Mark, the eldest, died. She never got over it. So Isaac, who is already sleeping with someone else, a woman called Genevieve who worked as his secretary, has Clarissa shoved in a room in the tower here.'

'Not in a hospital or something?'

'No chance, he doesn't want people hearing about it so he just hides her away. She's strapped up in a straightjacket, prisoner in her own home, fed by the servants. He got doctors to come and see her – they even tried electroconvulsive therapy on her –'

'Jesus!'

'I know, it was new then and did no good. Great life for her, locked up in her own house getting fried every week while her husband's downstairs shagging the secretary. Anyway, he also had another son, Thomas, but we'll talk about him later.'

'OK,' you say, 'let's keep looking around then.'

You move back into the corridor, directly facing you is a door marked 'Manager'.

'Worth a look?' asks Joe.

YES. GO TO 12.

NAH. GO TO 20.

29

'We may as well go all the way up to the top,' you tell Joe. 'If we're going to risk being in this thing let's make the most of it. As you say, up there the damage may not be so bad.'

'Fair enough.' Joe presses the button for the fourth floor and you film the two of you in the mirror, both trying to look braver than you actually feel.

A violent clunk and the lift judders – at which point you both pull a face that's far from brave – and then the lift starts climbing up.

'I thought we were going to drop then.' Joe admits.

'There's time yet.'

But the lift continues to climb, steady and slow, the light on the buttons illuminates the second, the third and finally the fourth floor.

'Right then,' says Joe, 'we survived.'

The lift door opens and you pull the concertina gate aside so you can both step out onto the top floor.

To the right a door with an 'Emergency Exit' sign leads, presumably to the backstairs. Joe points at it.

'I knew there'd be more stairs,' he says. 'Still, the lift works fine so we know we're OK to get back down.'

'Yeah, I'll remind you of that when it crashes next time we try and use it.'

'Grow a pair.' He grins.

You turn right and move along the corridor. All of the rooms are locked and you're wondering if coming up here hasn't been a massive waste of time. You're about to say as much when Joe calls you down to the end of the corridor.

GO TO 37.

30

You move back to the terrace, heading up some steps to what was once a pair of glass doors, an exit from the sun room at the rear of the hotel. The glass is shattered now and crunches under your feet as you step into the large room filled with dead potted plants and old garden furniture. Magazines have turned to pulp thanks to the rain that has come in from the holes in the roof. Piles of leaves gather around coffee tables and on top of mildewed sofa cushions. It's like someone has taken a posh lounge and then left it outside for a year. Basically, that's *exactly* what happened.

Joe moves towards another pair of double doors that lead from the sun room into the main building. He turns the enormous handle and there's a loud shriek of distorted wood but they stay firmly shut.

'Is it locked?' you ask.

'Pretty sure they're just stuck,' he says, bracing himself and pulling as hard as he can. The wood screeches again and then the doors swing open, sending Joe stumbling backwards, feet skidding on broken glass. You grab him and help him stay on his feet.

'Thanks mate,' he says, 'nearly had it right off the hinges.'

The two of you step into the hotel, a narrow corridor of damp carpet and blackened walls. The smell is musk and old smoke, rot and mould.

'It's not as burned out as I thought it might have been,' you say.

'Yeah, I told you, the damage is limited to a few places really. The first floor and the reception area are pretty bad I think but the rest should be safe enough.'

'Where should we go first do you think?' you ask him.

'I don't know, some of the bedrooms I guess?' he suggests.

'Makes sense. Did a lot of guests see weird stuff?'

GO TO 59 THEN COME RIGHT BACK HERE WHERE IT'S SAFER. NOT SAFE, OF COURSE, BUT SAFER.

'Yeah,' says Joe. 'A lot. And, you know, that's always been the point of these videos. I just wanna find actual proof that ghosts exists. So hopefully we're in the right place to get some answers.'

Right now, you're not even sure you want to be asking the question, but you go with it.

You're in the entrance foyer now and Joe was right, the fire damage here is much more obvious. Even in the semi-darkness, the smell alone is enough to tell you what happened here.

'May as well check the lights,' suggests Joe, 'they came on in here earlier after all.' He walks over to a wall panel of light switches and starts flipping them all on. The great hall ahead lights up – not completely, a lot of bulbs have blown, but enough to get a clearer sense of the place –

and it's a chaos of opulence that's had a sound kicking. The expensive furniture, the expensive paintings on the walls, the expensive rug in the middle of the floor... Blackened, bent, rotted, torn, smashed. It's not just the fire, it's the fact that everything was doused with the fireman's hoses and then left to fester. You can tell this place reeked of money once, but only just.

'Nice,' you say.

'Yeah,' Joe agrees, heading towards the stairs. 'It'll be even worse upstairs where the fire started.'

'Great.'

You look up and spot a security camera in the corner of the room. You point it out to Joe. 'How brilliant would it be if they had old footage from those that you could edit in?'

'That would be amazing, doubt they kept any of it though.'

You both move to the foot of the grand staircase and look up at the burned mess leading up to the next floor. One of the stairs has completely caved in, several others look like they're seriously considering it.

'You think it's safe?' you ask.

'Only one way to find out, geeza. We'll stick to the edges and see how far we can get. If it's looking like we can't do it we'll just come back down. We don't wanna die but it'd be bloody dumb to not give it a go. We'll go really slow and give up if it looks dangerous.'

That seems fair enough. Joe shoves his camera in his pocket and leads the way, stepping on the edge of the stairs where they'll be the most stable. The wood creaks a bit but seems OK. After he's gone a few steps you start to follow, holding your camera with one hand, using the other to steady yourself with the handrail.

You're almost halfway up and the only way to get past the broken stair is going to be to stretch your legs as wide as possible, get a foot on the higher stair so you're bridging the gap, then pull yourself up.

'It's not just one broken step,' says Joe, stretching his foot and testing the next one up, it gives a soft, crunching sound. 'The one after that isn't safe either. Hang about.' He readjusts his balance so he can stretch his leg past both of the unsafe stairs to the next in line. It creaks again. 'Shit,' he says, shuffling again so that he can reach the step after that. That seems more stable. 'I think it's fine,' he adds, 'we just have to skip three of them.'

Taking a firmer grip on the handrail he stretches his leg as far as he can, avoiding the three weak steps. 'Jesus!' he moans, 'I'm feeling very dodgy sensations in places I never have before. Give me your hand.'

You swap the camera from your left hand to your right so that you can stick your arm out and help push Joe up. He pulls on the handrail with one hand, pushing against your braced arm with the other. He wobbles a bit but, as his balance shifts over the broken stairs, he rights himself and clears the gap. The stair he's climbed onto creaks slightly, but no worse than most of the others. He steps up one more and then turns back to you.

'It's no problem,' he assures you, 'piece of piss. Give me your camera and then I'll help pull you up.'

You hand over the camera and get as close to the broken steps as you can. Then, keeping your right foot steady, you stretch out with your left, inching your hands along the handrail. Once you have a foot on both steps, you reach out to grab Joe's hand.

'Ready?' he asks. You nod.

 GO TO 14.

31

Isaac hadn't meant to kill her, these things just happen sometimes. If she'd just stood still, just realised when she'd gone too far, if she hadn't damn well *smiled* like that… But as his father had always said, 'If wishes were horses, beggars would ride.' She had done all of those things and he had reacted, which is why she was now at the bottom of the stairs while he was still standing at the top.

He wondered if the lover she so enjoyed bragging about would find her so alluring now.

Her lover.

Genevieve had had a few, he'd known that. And as long as she had kept it quiet, kept it professional if you like, she could have had many more as far as he was concerned. But no, she had to fall for that actor. Joseph Kledwell. An empty smile in a loud suit. Actors couldn't keep secrets, everyone knew that. A little marital infidelity was one thing, positively traditional in fact, but when one read about it in the gossip columns then… Well, steps had to be taken.

He'd have settled for an apology and her reassurance that she would avoid the attentions of Kledwell in future. That little bit of common sense and civility would have seen the matter closed. But no, she had claimed to love Kledwell. Had even suggested she wanted to leave Isaac for him. He hadn't believed the threat, telling Genevieve that she liked money too much. He was quite sure she'd never leave her comfortable lifestyle for an uncertain future alongside such a transient as Kledwell. Could she really imagine living alone in his tiny rooms in town, while he toured the country shouting at easily pleased strangers in the cheap seats? Kledwell's career was going nowhere. The best he could hope for was to keep crawling around the provinces shovelling out cheap thrillers and broad comedies in run-down theatres.

'He's had a lot of movie interest,' she had claimed. Isaac was quite sure Kledwell was far from the first actor deluded by his own possible potential to claim that.

No. He was going nowhere and he was poor. For Genevieve to give up all this for a lifestyle like that she'd have to really be in love with him and that, of course, was as absurd as the plots of those damned plays Kledwell acted in. Love? Ridiculous. There was no such thing.

In this, it turned out he was wrong. Genevieve, it seemed, loved Joseph Kledwell considerably and intended to pack up her belongings that very afternoon.

'Not all men are as dull and heartless as you, you know!' she had said.

Perhaps that was what had really been the deciding factor. Yes, he supposed it was. Heartless he could live with. It was true. But dull?

'There are more important things than money, Isaac,' she had added, offering him a patronising smile. 'If you'd discovered that a few years ago there might still be hope for you.'

He hadn't even been aware he was going to do it until he saw his hand held out in front of him and saw Genevieve's face turn from quietly patronising to terrified.

She had made such a noise as she'd fallen. Especially when she had crashed through the uprights of the bannister and flown directly from the third floor straight to the landing of the first.

Now look at her. Everything pointing the wrong way. Absurd. Like a clothes dummy waiting to be assembled.

He sighed. He really did seem to have terrible luck with his wives. Still, at least this one wouldn't continue to clutter up the place.

He began shouting in feigned panic. 'Someone! Quickly! She's fallen! Call an ambulance!'

Then he made his way down to where Genevieve's body lay, wondering how much it was going to cost to repair the bannister.

GO TO 64.

'Let's just keep climbing,' you say. 'We may as well start at the top and then make our way back down.'

'Fair enough.'

You head up the last few flights of stairs and step out onto a long corridor lined with numbered rooms. On the walls, more ugly paintings leer at you as you walk along trying the doors.

'Locked,' you say, trying your third door.

'I'm bloody livid mate,' admits Joe, 'I never thought about that. Hotel room doors lock automatically don't they? I should have asked if there were any keycards or something. There's probably a master that works for the lot.'

'Maybe it's down by reception? Behind the desk or something? Or in the manager's office.'

'Yeah maybe,' he nods. 'It's so long to have to go all the way back down and look though isn't it?'

'Yeah,' you agree. 'You'd think that some of the doors would have been left half-open, you know, when people ran out of here because of the fire.'

'You'd hope. Thing is, the hotel was struggling wasn't it? The place wouldn't have been booked out, so maybe they only let out rooms lower down, to save having to come up here all the time.'

'Makes sense.' You look up and see another of those security cameras staring down at you. Even though you know nobody looks at them anymore, there's something about a security camera. That dead lens, gazing at you. It's like being watched.

'I think we'll have to go back down,' you say, 'try the third floor?'

'Hang about…' calls Joe, who's moved down the far end of the corridor. 'This might be good.'

There's a pair of double doors, a plaque next to them saying 'Roof Lounge'. Joe tries the door, it's open.

'Here we go,' he says, 'it ain't over yet, geeza.'

GO TO 58.

It's terrible to imagine what Issac's wife must have gone through in this room. It certainly wouldn't have looked so luxurious then. Just for a moment you imagine this place with all the expensive furnishings stripped out. You imagine that poor woman, bound up in her straightjacket and left to rot.

'What happened to her?' you ask.

'Clarissa? She lived in here for ten years.'

'Ten years? In one room?'

'Yep. She eventually caught some kind of infection and died.'

'An infection? After everything she just dies of an infection?'

'Yeah, she was probably relieved, I know I would have been. Trapped in here with nothing but your own skull for company. If she wasn't mentally ill when they put her in here she certainly was in the end.'

'Horrible.'

For a minute, both of you just stare into space, looking at the room and imagining. Then something occurs to you.

'How did Isaac die?'

'No idea,' says Joe. 'It's the weirdest thing. It's like he vanishes. I looked everywhere, trying to find more information on him. I could see when this place was sold off, I could see what happened to everyone else in the family, but Isaac himself? Nothing. I even contacted the General Register Office. They have no record of a death certificate.' He grins. 'Maybe he's still here!'

'Ha ha,' you reply, in a deadpan voice, because that's not a thought you want in your head. 'Well, however he died, I hope it was horrible, after what he did to Clarissa. He deserves the worst. Stuck here all that time, nobody showing her any kindness at all.'

Joe nods, then has an idea.

'We should try and talk to her.'

You know what he's suggesting and the idea terrifies you. Still, if you're going to try and contact any of the spirits here you'd rather it was someone you had sympathy for.

'I suppose we could give it a go.'

'Let's make some space.'

The two of you push some of the furniture towards the walls so you've made a clear space on the floor. Sitting down, Joe opens his rucksack and pulls out the Ouija board and a glass.

'You know I hate that thing, right?' you tell him.

'Don't say that, we want this to be a positive thing. A chance to reach out and talk to Clarissa Godling in the hope she's found peace.'

'Yeah, OK.' You see his point. You're not sure you believe the Ouija board even does anything. You've used it before and you've never been quite convinced that it's not just people moving the glass. In fact sometimes you know that's what it is, people messing about, wanting to make something exciting out of nothing. You've read up on it though and apparently people can even do that subconsciously. That's also what can happen at those shows mediums do some times. You have a packed theatre, a message supposedly coming through, you want it to be for you, you're desperate for it to be for you, so you say all the right things. You don't want to admit that when the medium tells you that your Aunt Gladys says you always liked raspberries, that you have no idea what they're talking about. You've never had a strong feeling about a raspberry in your life. Because if you admit that, it's all over, you've seen how it works. 'Oh,' the medium will say, 'it looks like I'm receiving someone new then, does that mean anything to anyone else here? Raspberries? Who really like raspberries as a kid?' 'Me!' someone will shout and that's that, the conversation's with them now and your chance to talk to the person you've lost would be gone. So you just agree, desperate to keep the conversation going. Desperate for all this to be real.

With the Ouija board your subconscious is guiding your fingers, trying to build stories out of the movement, trying to make it all be real, trying to have it all make sense.

That's what you've read.

But you're not sure you entirely believe it.

Joe puts the Ouija board on the floor between you and places the glass on top of it. You put your cameras on either side of you, as high up as you can, looking down on the board so they can record clearly what happens.

'Right then,' he says, 'are you ready?'

'I suppose so,' you reply.

And you both put your fingers on the glass.

 GO TO 56.

You turn left along the corridor. You push through a pair of fire doors and, once again, the damage is more obvious. A bust of an old Roman has turned black on its charred plinth, a couple of paintings have been turned into modern art, their canvases black and torn while the sooty frames still stand. The floor is sticky, the carpet in patches. A large potted plant is now nothing but an eruption of dark twigs, its pot cracked, spilling guts of earth onto the stained floor.

There are a pair of double doors on your right and you step through them, the lights work in here and reveal a large library. From floor to ceiling, the walls are filled with bookshelves, row after row of books. Here and there are dotted armchairs and coffee tables. The doors obviously stopped the fire getting too serious in here, you can only imagine how this place would have gone up if a spark had got into it, every single one of those books was an inferno waiting to happen.

You move along one of the bookcases, looking at their spines. Most of them are old, there's nothing you recognise.

'You think this was Isaac's actual library?' you ask, pulling a book off the shelf and looking at the cover. It has a ram's head on it, the title reads: *Ancient Magick – A Concordance.*

'Who knows mate?' Joe replies, searching one of the other shelves. 'Could have been I suppose.'

'I don't think you normally have weird shit like this in a hotel,' you say, flipping through the book. It's like a guide book to magic spells, curses, rituals… really mad stuff. It's written in such an old-fashioned, weird style.

'Listen to this,' you tell Joe, starting to read, '"Take the roots of the *Laburnicus Clothidae* but only when the sabbath is due and the moon is waxing in the firmament. Grind the roots to a paste with the lifeblood of an Ox and smear the paste upon thine breast."'

'Very naughty,' says Joe. 'Why would you be doing that then?'

You look at the chapter title. 'So you can "Augment the Sacred Strength of your Heart and Lungs".'

'Oh yeah,' says Joe, 'sounds pretty good. Anything in there for penis enlargement? Asking for a mate.'

'Probably have to stick it in a donkey or something,' you reply, 'but only when the moon is full and there's two Thursdays in a week.'

You put the book back on the shelf and move further along. 'Loads of these books are about black magic and stuff,' you tell him, 'it's mental.'

'This section's all about history,' says Joe, picking up a book. 'Old wars and stuff.' Suddenly he has an idea. 'We should do a spell.'

'What?' You really don't like the sound of this much. You feel like you're pushing your luck in here as it is.

'Come on mate, it'll be sick. It's a load of cobblers anyway. I'm not smearing myself with anything though. Is there something easier?'

You pick the book back up again and flick through. 'No idea, there's loads of stuff here.'

'Let's have a look.' He takes the book off you and sits down in one of the armchairs, a big cloud of dust erupting from around him. 'Lovely,' he says, coughing slightly.

'Dust is mainly dead human skin,' you tell him, 'you do know that, don't you?'

'Oi nah,' he replies, 'So I'm just currently covered in dead people.'

He starts flicking through the book. 'Flying? Yeah! Oh, you need chicken hearts. Got any chicken hearts?'

'I've got a protein bar and a bottle of water.'

'Chicken-heart-flavour protein bar?'

'Blueberry, you knob.'

'No good then.' He carries on flicking through. 'We need one that's just, you know, something that doesn't require throwing a load of bloody animal guts at the thing. I didn't know magic spells were so much like cooking. What about my next YouTube video being: "Cooking my Friend an Evil Curse Prank".'

He discovered that it was his bank that had given the mortgage on the hotel and had now taken ownership. Was there such a thing as fate? It seemed too perfect.

His boss had been uncomfortable about letting him handle the account. She had thought it morbid. Julian had convinced her that it would give him exactly the sort of closure he needed. To be able to sell the building on, see it torn down. It would finally help him move on. Eventually she had agreed and Julian had sat at his desk, the keys to the property in his hand. Well now, wasn't this an opportunity?

He had watched the Joe Weller videos again. Might this be interesting? Send him into the hotel, let him stir things up? See if he discovered anything? If he did then Julian would at least have the answer to one of his most pressing questions, the question he asked himself whenever he had one of those night-time visits from the girlfriend he had killed: 'Am I mad?'

He had arranged it. Probably nothing would happen. Probably. But if it did, he would be there.

In his free time he had visited the building, trying to get the power back on, the phone, trying to prepare. He'd spent money on updating the security cameras, channelling the feed into one of the empty rooms on the top floor.

It hadn't taken long to sort it. Controlling the account, he had found it easy enough to do it all on the sly. And soon, of course, the bulldozers would wipe out any evidence of his interference. Yes, it was perfect. He would sit there in the upstairs room and watch what happened. He would see if Katy really was still there, if she was still dangerous. He would see what company she was really keeping these days.

And he would find out if he was mad.

At least that part worked out OK.

IF YOU RAN FROM JULIAN ON THE GROUND FLOOR, GO TO 47.

IF YOU AND JOE MET HIM ON THE THIRD FLOOR STAIRS, GO TO 51.

36

Walking along the corridor, you both jump as, once again, you hear a phone ringing. The sound of it, echoing along these abandoned corridors is weirdly unsettling. Despite the fixtures and furniture still being in place, this is clearly a dead building and having a noise so piercing, so part of the living world, bursting in feels like someone laughing hysterically during a funeral.

'There's probably still listings for the hotel online,' you say, 'people are trying to book a room, not knowing it's long gone.'

'Yeah, probably,' Joe agrees.

The phone stops ringing and you're glad.

'Hang about.' Joe stops and looks up at a framed portrait on the wall. It's the portrait of a young man. He's sort of handsome, like an old-fashioned movie star, but the fire damage has worked an act of grotesque graffiti on it. Originally the subject was leaning in front of an old fireplace. The soot has blanked out most of the background though, but some of the flames from the fire are still visible. It now looks like the picture of a young man relaxing casually in Hell.

'I recognise that face,' Joe says.

There's a small plaque underneath the picture: 'Thomas Godling'.

'Isaac's second son.' Joe nods to himself now he's remembering why the face was familiar.

'You said you'd tell me about him later,' you say. 'Did he go into the family business? Flog a few machine guns to people?'

'No,' Joe replies, 'he's kind of a mystery actually, because there's no proof.'

'Proof of what?'

GO TO 46.

"HANG ABOUT...
I RECOGNISE
THAT FACE."

There's a pair of double doors, slightly ajar, and you step through them into what can only be a private suite.

'Wow,' says Joe, flipping on the light switches and panning the camera around the room.

A four-poster bed surrounded by hanging curtains is pressed against the back wall. At its foot is an ornate vanity table, painted gold, the frame around the mirror as thick and ornate as something you'd expect to see wrapped around a priceless oil painting. To the right of the bed, a bay window, looking out over the estate, the curved stone ledge in front of it turned into a bench by padded cushions, a small coffee table placed in the arc formed by the bench. On the table is a display of flowers now dry and dead.

In the far corner a small set of steps leads up again, presumably to the bathroom.

'This place is nice.' Joe throws himself down on the bed. A cloud of dust erupts around him. 'Could do with a bloody clean though.'

You head to the window, but with the light inside it's just a wall of blackness. You can't see anything.

'Nice,' you agree. 'But you know where this is?'

'Oh,' says Joe, realising, 'the tower… yeah… where Isaac put his wife Clarissa.'

 GO TO 13.

It's only a short drop from the terrace to the gravel path around the building, so you both hop over rather than wasting time running for the steps.

'Hey, wait a minute!' Joe shouts towards the retreating figure as you both leave the gravel path and push on across the overgrown garden. 'We just want to talk!'

If the running man hears you he certainly doesn't care. You can't see him anymore but you can hear him clearly enough as he pushes through the branches ahead.

'Mate!' Joe shouts again. 'Seriously, we just want to ask you about the hotel that's all.'

'It's no good,' you say, knowing you're never going to catch up with whoever it is. 'He's getting too far ahead. He obviously knows his way around the place.'

You both stop running and all is quiet. Either the man has stopped running too or he's reached open ground and is now legging it as fast as he can.

'Worth a try,' says Joe. 'Shall we head back?'

You nod and the two of you turn around and head back through the undergrowth towards the hotel.

'What do you think scared him?' you ask.

'Oh who bloody knows? Like you said, he probably thought we were official people or something, going to have a go at him for being here.'

Which would make sense but you can't help but remember that the man didn't seem to be looking at you when he freaked out. It was hard to tell in the low light, you couldn't see his face, but from the angle of his shadow he was looking higher than that. He was looking up at the building. Did he see something at a window? Surely it was too dark for that. But then you start thinking again about the lights coming on and the idea that there may be someone else inside the building. You were both hoping that if there *had* been someone inside it was this guy you'd been chasing, but what if it wasn't? What if the person who had been switching on the lights was still inside?

The bushes seem thicker on your way back and it's getting hard to push your way through.

'Is this the way we came?' you ask.

'I thought it was,' Joe replies, shining the light from the camera around and finding nothing but foliage, 'I mean, we pretty much ran in a straight line from the building didn't we?'

You did, but this is getting ridiculous, you're now fighting to take each step, branch after branch holding you back.

'I think we need to turn around again,' you suggest, 'getting through this is just impossible.'

'Yeah,' Joe agrees, and the two of you shift around to come back the way you've just come. Which should be easy, right? Because you've already cut a path by forcing your way through it. So why is it just as hard to move that way?

'This is stupid,' you say, branches tugging at your jacket, 'I'm all caught up.'

'Hang about.' Joe starts moving over to unhook you. Except he can't, because he's caught too.

'Christ,' he moans, the material of his hoodie tearing as he tries to pull his arm forward. 'I can't get my sodding arm free.'

The bushes thrash and rustle as you both try and pull yourselves loose but neither of you are going anywhere. Breathless, angry, you stop pulling for a minute and so does Joe. But you can still hear the bushes rustling. Is someone else coming?

'Maybe that bloke's come back again?' Joe says.

But then you realise, as impossible as it is, that the only thing moving here are the bushes themselves. The branches growing, twisting, creaking. The more they move, the more you're stuck. It's as if the plants want to hold onto you, to keep you, to crush you. Which is just stupid. Crazy. Impossible.

You're still fighting against the idea when you feel the thin, pointed twigs push into your mouth, up your nose, wrapping around your face. You try and shout to Joe, but the leaves are filling your mouth and all you can do is make useless, gagging sounds. The same sounds you can hear from Joe, just a few feet away.

You're blind now, completely cocooned in the branches. You're still wondering how this can be happening when the branches begin to pull and the cracking and tearing sounds really start.

OK, so now you've learned something. The choices you make don't always work out well. This building is dangerous. Forget what you believe is possible. Forget the rules. You might not get out of here alive. So watch your step, choose carefully and maybe you'll live through this.

**NOW GO TO 26,
WHICH IS WHAT
YOU SHOULD HAVE
DONE EARLIER.**

39

You walk back past the places you've already been, mentally ticking them off as you pass. The dining room, the kitchen, the conference rooms…

The place is built like a maze, corridors looping back on themselves, cutting from one place to another. At one point you hear the phone ring again but you ignore it this time.

'Some bastards never learn do they?' says Joe.

He opens another door, and peers inside. 'Games room!' he cries, going in and flicking on the lights.

There's a pool table in the middle of the room, a bookcase filled with paperback novels, and a chessboard still set up to play.

'Any good at chess?' Joe asks.

'Nah, I'll take you on at pool though.'

Joe is moving around the pool table. 'No balls,' he says.

'I know,' you reply, 'but you try your best.'

'Shut up.' He grins. 'That's well annoying, I could have smashed you at a game.'

'Other way around, mate, other way around.'

Above the fireplace there's a portrait of Isaac Godling, his miserable face everything you don't want in a room that's supposed to be fun.

'What happened to Isaac?' you ask. 'How did he die?'

'It's the weirdest thing,' Joe replies, 'I have no idea. I looked everywhere but there's no mention of him dying. I even contacted the General Register Office, tried to find when his death was registered. They had no record of it.'

'How's that work?' you wonder, 'we know what happened to all of them, the whole family, and we know he outlived them all but… well, he must have died of something!'

'Yeah, all I know is that he seems to have lived here on his own for a few years and then the house was sold on in the late sixties and turned into a hotel. He must have died around then I guess.' Joe grins, 'Or he's still here!'

There's a small table set between a pair of armchairs. On the table there's a particularly horrible-looking ornament of a clenched knight's fist, holding a small mace.

'Nice,' says Joe. 'Spiky ornaments of death. Though if it's to scale that's one seriously small knight.'

'Sir Midget of the Tiny Table.'

'Knight of the Mini Realm.'

'Sir Notalot.'

There's a drawer in the side of the table. Joe opens it and pulls out a pack of cards.

'Time for a magic trick!' he shouts, 'You saw my walking on water video, right?'

He pulls the cards out of the pack and makes to shuffle them, they fly everywhere. A shower of playing cards rains down onto the pool table.

'Right then,' he heads back towards the door, 'I wonder if anyone ever banged in here?' Joe asks himself.

'You are literally the most dodgy geeza on the planet, mate.' You shake your head.

'Like surely someone has… anyways, let's move on,' Joe says.

GO TO 63.

You walk along the rest of the corridor but most of the other rooms are closed, their doors locked.

'Should have thought to check behind the reception desk to see if there was a master key or something,' admits Joe. 'I just didn't think about it.'

'I didn't either,' you reply, 'so don't beat yourself up over it.'

You're back at the main staircase. Joe looks up. 'To be honest, mate,' he says, 'I think they look safe enough. What do you think?'

You think you don't like the idea of using either the staircase or the lift, but you have to admit, given a choice the stairs win. The fire, the smoke and heat rising, has left its mark up here but it's mainly cosmetic. You rub your hand on the carpet and it's singed and melted, hard stubble, the weave underneath showing through. The walls are covered in soot, great streaks of it rising up the staircase. You can imagine what it must have been like here with the fire raging a couple of floors below. It would have been like standing in a chimney, great, choking clouds of smoke rising towards the top of the house.

You climb up the first couple of stairs, testing them to see if they feel solid.

'I think it's fine,' you say. 'Let's just get on with it.'

You're halfway up when the lights go out. There wasn't much light to begin with, with so many bulbs blown, but you only appreciate something when it's gone.

'Shit,' Joe mutters, reaching out for the bannister. 'Mind your step, we'll be alright.'

'Knowing the electrics here they'll probably come back on in a minute,' you say.

You shine the camera lights on the stairs in front of you as you continue to climb.

Turning to take the second flight up towards the fourth floor you feel something brush past you. You freeze.

'I felt something,' you say, swinging the light around, trying to see what it was that touched you.

'What do you mean you felt something?' Joe asks before shouting and snatching his hand away from the bannister.

'What?' you ask.

'Something just grabbed my hand,' he says. 'I'm sure it did. Like someone was walking up the stairs behind me, reached forward and slapped their hand down over mine.'

'There's nothing here.'

You're moving the light up and down the stairs, desperate to catch sight of whatever it is that you now think is on these stairs with you. Then something touches you again. It feels like a hand poking you in the ribs. You act automatically, lashing out with your fist and, just for a second, it feels like you actually connect with something. Actually *punch* someone.

'What was it?' Joe asks, turning his camera and shining the light on you. 'There's nothing there.'

'Nothing we can *see*,' you reply. 'Get moving would you?'

He nods and you both start running up the stairs.

You manage a few steps before something trips you up and you slam down against that melted carpet, winding yourself slightly on the edge of one of the stairs. Joe grabs you and pulls you back onto your feet.

'Keep moving!' he shouts and both of you sprint the last few steps onto the fourth floor landing.

The lights come back on and, as you knew was the case, you can clearly see you're alone up there.

'What the hell was that?' you ask. 'We both felt something, yeah? Like there was someone else on the stairs with us?'

Joe nods, his face pale. 'But there wasn't.' He points. 'There's nothing there.'

You both stare at the empty stairwell and slowly, your nerves get back under control.

'We imagined it didn't we?' you say. 'We've got ourselves so wound up we actually thought there was something there.'

'I guess,' he agrees, rubbing his face. You can tell he's not convinced. In all honesty, neither are you, but now the lights are back on, now you're off those stairs, it's hard to hold onto the fear. There's nothing there. Neither of you saw anything. You read loads of stories about people becoming so convinced of something that isn't real that they end up believing it. Hell, Derren Brown's made a bloody career out of it. Part of you's always scoffed at it in the past. Not anymore. You say as much to Joe.

He nods. 'You must be right,' he says, and you can see he's relaxing a bit. 'This place is just getting to us.'

The corridor stretches to either side of the stairs. You aim to the right and make your way past more locked rooms, Joe was right about that damn key, please don't say you're going to have to go down those stairs again.

'We're in luck,' says Joe, pointing to the end of the corridor.

 GO TO 37.

'Why is that woman screaming all the time?' asks the next man in line, his hair wild and sticking out in all directions, his skin burned and peeling. He smiles and you see several of his teeth are missing. 'At least I won't have to sit through tomorrow's meeting.'

'Julian?' asks a woman wearing nothing but soap suds and confusion, her skin so wrinkled she looks twice her age. 'Has anyone seen my bastard of a boyfriend?'

'I'll help you look,' offers a man, also naked, swatting away at the flies buzzing around his head, 'tell me, do you come here often?'

'Listen to him try and be charming,' says the young man who follows, sipping at a tumbler of whisky. You recognise this one. This is Thomas Godling. The dangerous Thomas Godling. 'What can I say? You've either got it or you haven't.' His face falls. 'Not that it matters. Not in the end.'

And you realise what this is, just as Thomas Godling is followed by a woman whose whole head is a raging ball of flame, a candle in a business suit that's screaming at you. 'You shouldn't be here! This is my home! Mine!'

These are the dead of Priory Grange. And one by one as they file in you start to put names to some of the faces. But the main one, the important one, comes last.

'Oh Christ! says Joe. 'There's no way this is happening? We must be dreaming or something. Is that what this is? Are we dreaming?'

If it is a dream, here is the man who is dreaming it: Isaac Godling, with his thin face and wispy hair, his large nose and that wide grin that's altogether too full of teeth.

'You came here,' he says, pushing his way past the crowd of the dead, 'wanting answers.'

He walks up to you and Joe.

'You came here wanting to know.' You wouldn't have ever thought that smile could grow wider, and yet it does. 'Is there life after death?' he asks. 'Can the dead still walk?'

He leans in close. 'It's a good question. Allow me to answer it for you.'

And then there is only darkness and the sound of you and Joe screaming.

'Sometimes,' Tom Salinsky thought, as he took off his shoes and sat down heavily on the bed, 'you just want to punch a day right in its stupid face.'

He hated these corporate weekends, with their stupid wall charts, stupid sales awards and stupid name badges. (Honestly, how hard was it to spell 'Salinsky' anyway? How did you manage to squeeze two 'z's in there without being a complete moron?)

I mean, yeah, fine, it was a nice enough hotel, better than some he'd been to over the last few years. But, what was the use of a nice hotel if you couldn't make the most of it? Not like he was able relax was it? They crammed so much into these conferences that the only time you had off was the evening and even that filled up thanks to everyone having to eat together.

He'd been sat next to Bryan from the Colchester office this evening, a man whose crimes against gravy had to be seen to be believed. After that it was straight to the bar and if you tried to cry off, you never heard the end of it. Not that Tom didn't like a drink but once Paul Farley from head office started the drinking games it was all Tom could do not to brain the loud bastard with a stool. There was having a drink with your mates and then there was trying to neck a pint while passing an inflatable sex doll to someone using only your feet. Laugh? No. He hadn't.

So he'd got away as soon as he could, and was now sitting with a buzzing noise in his head in a hotel room that would be perfectly nice as long as it promised not to start spinning in the very near future. Which it would. Of course it would. At which point he'd be able to enjoy the perfectly nice bathroom and its perfectly nice toilet bowl.

God, he hated it.

If he could just try and stay awake for a bit. Drink some water, or work his way through those disgusting sachets of instant coffee. Yes, that was the key to surviving this. Take the little tray of coffee sachets, packs of biscuits and the couple of small bottles of water and neck the lot. Hopefully pouring that on the bubbling mess of booze in his system would take the edge off his drunkenness enough to let him sleep (preferably without losing tonight's 'pan-seared salmon with fine beans and sun-dried tomatoes' down the u-bend).

He staggered towards the tray on the desk, grabbing the biscuits first and shoving them one by one into his mouth like a man desperately feeding a vending machine with coins. Then he drank the first bottle of water while taking the small travel kettle to the bathroom. He filled it, and moved back to the desk where the power sockets were. Frankly, he was kind of tired after all that and wondered if he could manage to move anymore. He felt like he'd run a frigging marathon.

'Come on, Tommo,' Paul Farley's voice said in his head, and he could picture the grinning idiot, pretending to hump the sex doll in front of one of the staff, 'put your bloody back into it!'

He was fighting to get the kettle's plug in the wall when the TV came on, volume far too loud, making him jump and fumble with the kettle. It tipped up on the desk, spilling water over a folder of sales notes he was supposed to present the following morning.

'Shitting balls,' he mumbled, righting the kettle, snatching his notes off the desk and then bobbing in confusion as he tried to decided what to do next. His brain was like a buffering video connection, his mental bandwidth exceeded by having to think about the TV, the kettle, his sales notes and the fact that he wasn't entirely sure those bastard biscuits weren't already thinking about crawling back up from his stomach.

The TV first. It was so loud it was probably disturbing the other guests and the last thing he needed was to end up fielding complaints from the front desk. The *very* last thing he wanted right now was to have to speak to another human. That was beyond him.

If he's right, if it really is more dangerous to stop, what choice do you have?

'OK,' you say. 'But only to close the conversation. Alright? Just to make it safe.'

'OK,' he agrees, nodding at your empty chair, 'sit down.'

You head back to your chair, sit down and reach towards the glass. For a second your fingers hover a short distance away, you can't believe you're going through with this. Then, swearing under your breath, you place your fingers gently on the glass opposite Joe's.

'Right,' says Joe. 'We're sorry about that, but it was too much. Was that a lot of you? We can't talk to you all at once. It has to be just one of you.'

The glass stays still and you're really hoping it never moves again. But it does. Slowly, almost as if it's embarrassed, the glass slides towards YES.

'Thank you,' says Joe, 'so this is just one spirit now?'

The glass moves away from YES, just a few centimetres and then slides back.

'Good,' says Joe, 'thank you.'

'So we can say goodbye then?' you ask, prompting Joe more than anything.

The glass, quicker this time, insistent, moves to 'NO.'

'Oh Christ,' you whisper.

The glass moves towards the letters.

I. M. P. O. R. T. A. N. T.

'You have to tell us something important?' asks Joe.

The glass moves to YES.

'Important for you or important for us?' you ask.

'Good question,' Joe mutters.

Y. O. U. the glass spells. D. A. N. G. E. R.

'Oh Jesus,' you moan, 'I really can't do this.'

'You have to,' says Joe, 'you saw what it said.' Then, to the spirit. 'We're in danger?'

The glass moves to YES.

It occurs to you again that this might all be Joe. You really hope it is. Please let it all be Joe.

'Are you doing this?' you ask him. 'I don't care if you are. Actually, that's not true. I really hope you are.'

'I swear mate,' he says, 'this isn't me.'

You glance at the camera, wondering how terrified you look right now on the footage. Not because you're embarrassed by it but because you genuinely haven't ever been this scared in your life and you wonder what that looks like. What do you look like when you're scared half to death?

'Why are we in danger?' Joe asks.

'Who are we in danger from?' you ask.

'One question at a time, mate,' Joe reminds you.

'Fine,' you sigh, 'sorry.'

Joe repeats your question. 'Who are we in danger from?'

The glass starts to spell out a word again: J. U. L. I.

GO TO 27.

home. He'd never suspect that Thom had picked her up from the bus stop and driven her to a 'lovely little pub I know over Hawkhurst way'.

Of course, when they got there, she didn't really know what she wanted to drink, stumbling awkwardly over all his suggestions and trying to imagine what a lady of distinction – rather than an eighteen-year-old country girl from the post office – might like. She eventually plumped for a port and lemon.

She sipped at it and told him everything. He asked so many questions! Wanting to know all about her, about her friends (that didn't take long); her plans (neither did that); where she saw herself being in ten years time (stuck in the same old village, doing the same boring things).

'Well,' he said eventually, 'I suppose I really should see about getting you home.'

'I suppose so,' she admitted, stumbling ever so slightly as she got up from the table.

They headed out into the cold night, the wind immediately wiping away the effect of at least one of her drinks as it blasted her towards his little sports car.

'Foul night,' Thom muttered and, for a moment she panicked, then she realised he was just talking about the weather. 'Much more of this and I shall have to consider popping abroad. I can only take so much lacklustre rain.' He smiled. 'A good storm, a real belter, nothing wrong with that. But weather that just sits there, heavy and dull and damp and pointless. Give me the south of France any day.'

Jane had never been to France. She had never even left the county and cautiously admitted as much as they climbed into the car.

'Well,' said Thom, pulling on his driving gloves and turning the ignition, 'maybe we shall have to see about that.'

She had no idea what to say, terrified that whatever reply she offered might break it.

'I've had a lovely evening,' he said after a brief pause. 'Have you?'

'Oh yes,' she said, perhaps rather too quickly. 'Lovely.'

'Good,' he nodded, 'that's good.'

They drove in silence for a short while, Thom going perhaps a little faster than she might have liked – though she would never have dared mention it, she knew men didn't like being criticised over their driving. Jane looked out of the window at the trees flashing by, the light of the moon blinking between them. It made her think of a film reel, hand-cranked, turning the real world into a series of flashing, juddering images.

Suddenly, Thom turned off the road, driving the car along a track that cut deeper into the woods.

'Don't worry,' he said, 'there's just something I need to do. You trust me don't you?'

Jane may not have left the county but she'd read enough books and been to the pictures often enough to know that men who asked if they had your trust didn't deserve it, but she was feeling so dreamy, so happy, she just nodded.

'Good,' he replied, pulling the car to a halt. For a moment he just sat there, staring out of the window.

'Are you alright?' she asked after a few seconds.

'No,' he admitted, 'I don't think I probably am.'

He got out of the car, closing the door behind him and walked a little way ahead. She watched him, lit up in the beam of the headlights, the wind whipping his jacket and tie. What should she do? What was wrong? They had been having such a nice time. Had it been something she said? Or didn't say? Maybe he thought she was rude for not replying to his comment about France.

She got out of the car.

Walking up behind him, she still didn't know what to say. How to try and make him better. But she had to say something.

'I wish I could help,' she said, putting her hand on his arm.

'Help?' he asked.

'With whatever's wrong.'

He nodded. 'Difficult though isn't it? How do I make myself better? Doing what I want to do will make me *feel* better, certainly. It always does. It makes me feel… *wonderful.*' He put such emphasis on that last word, as if no word in the English language could quite manage to express how strong his feelings were. 'But it's wrong,' he continued, 'that's the problem, old girl, it's so… so wrong. So should I stop myself? Should I try and resist?'

'I… I don't know.' Jane still wasn't worried. It still didn't occur to her that her life was in danger. Why would it? Thom Godling was such a lovely man. 'What is it that you want to do?'

He made a strange noise then, like a toddler expressing agony without language. 'I think I'll just have to show you,' he said, finally, and took her by the throat.

Later, driving back, happy despite the considerable ache in his fingers and arms from their overuse, Thom once again thought about going to the south of France. Yes, he thought, a break is what I need. A change of scenery. A few weeks just to really be myself.

When Jane's body was eventually found he would be sitting on a beach at Saint-Tropez, enjoying the feel of the sun on his skin. When the body was identified – some few days later, he had left very little that was obviously recognisable – he had already moved on to Aix-en-Provence. When Jane's parents answered the door to the sad face of the village policeman, he was eating sole in a restaurant just along from the cathedral. The fish was a trifle overdone but the excellent wine more than made up for it.

GO TO 19.

47

You're running.

You need to think, to come up with some kind of plan of action, but that's hard because…

You're running and he's right behind you.

Right now all you know is that Joe has a chance. As hard as Julian hit him, he was groaning and moving slightly, he was down but not out. He might be able to call someone. Or come and help. And if not, you'll think of something, you have to, because…

You're running and he's right behind you and he's laughing.

And it won't be the first time will it? Because you talked to someone that knows exactly what Julian's capable of, talked to someone who learned that lesson the hard way. God, you hope you don't end up talking to her again, all dead together.

You cross the reception – almost, but not quite, tripping over the toppled plinth that the horse statue had once sat on – and race out of the front door.

But now what? Which way to run? You have to think quickly because…

You're running and he's right behind you and he's laughing and he wants to kill you.

RUN TOWARDS THE DRIVEWAY AND THE EXIT BEYOND? GO TO 65. RUN TOWARDS THE GARDEN AND THE MAZE? GO TO 52.

'Julian?' you ask, looking at Joe. 'Do you know a Julian connected with this place?'

He shakes his head. 'Never heard of him.'

The glass moves again. G.O.

'Bloody right,' you say.

You can tell Joe is slightly reluctant, this has always been so important to him, to get proof of the supernatural, he's not sure he wants to let it go. But how much more proof does he need?

'You heard what it said,' you tell him, 'we should leave.'

'I guess,' he says, and then louder, 'Thank you for speaking to us. We leave now in peace.'

You snatch your fingers away from the glass, and, after a second so does he.

'That was amazing,' he says, glancing towards the cameras. 'I know what you're probably all thinking,' he tells the camera,. 'That we made all that up. That we were just putting on a show or something.'

'No show,' you agree, impatient. 'And you can add this in during editing, pack the tripods away, let's get out of here.'

He stares at the camera for another second or two then nods. He gets up, takes the camera off the tripod and starts packing it away. You do the same with the other one.

'Who do you think Julian is?' he asks.

'I hope we never find out.'

He shakes his head, exasperated. 'I don't know how you can be so willing to just leave without knowing.'

'You heard what it said, Joe. Danger. I'll be honest with you, I've never been convinced about the Ouija board, the ghosts and all that stuff but if that *was* genuine…'

'Idiot,' says Julian, 'you're filming this? Even now? You're obsessed!' He laughs and it's high and hysterical and awful. 'Nobody's going to be seeing any more of your little videos, haven't you realised that yet? I'm not letting you get out of here alive.'

'Mate, this is live streaming,' says Joe, 'people are watching it right now.' He glances at the screen. 'Nine thousand and forty three people currently live. Ooh…' He grins. 'Comment from someone called McGill94… "Who is this guy? Joe should just kick him in the bollocks."' Joe shrugs. 'The geeza's got a point.'

'Turn it off!' Julian screams, striding towards you both as you back away down the corridor.

'Hey!' Joe shouts. 'Back up Julian! I told you, this is live. You really want this many people as witnesses? How do you think you're getting out of that? Oh another comment…' He reads it. 'BuxtonArmy678 just telling me that they've called the police – so have loads of people by the look of it – apparently they're on their way.'

Julian stops moving, panic and confusion crossing his face as he looks at you both.

You glance at the screen. 'That's nice,' you say, 'GossJam reckons this should be your best video yet.'

'He might be right there,' says Joe. He looks at Julian. 'Don't be a dickhead mate, you're done. The only chance you've got is to run. You probably won't get far but you can try.'

Julian hesitates for another second, his grip on the pikestaff tightening. You can see he's desperately trying to think of a way out of this. But what option has he?

He turns and runs.

GO TO 66.

"DON'T BE A DICKHEAD MATE, YOU'RE DONE."

52

There's no point in running towards the gate, you haven't got the keys to let yourself out, they're still in Joe's pocket. Your only hope is to head into the garden, maybe lose Julian in the maze. It's as good a place as any to hide, with a bit of luck you may even be able to double back to the house, check on Joe and then lock you both in one of the rooms until you can get the police to come.

Your camera's still in your hand but you're not thinking about the mad, shaky footage you're getting right now. Later – if you're lucky – it'll be a terrifying thing to have captured, you running for your life. Right now the camera's nothing but a torch.

Behind you, you hear Julian stumble, he hits the ground with a pained cry and you hear the pikestaff dig into the grass. Is it worth turning and running back at him? Maybe you could beat him while he's down, possibly even grab the weapon off him? But if you don't, if you're a fraction too slow, then you've blown it, he'll stab you with that thing and you'll have lost the one chance at this you have. No, you keep running, at least you can get ahead slightly, give yourself room to move.

The maze is directly ahead and you switch the camera off. You can see the entrance, you don't need the light anymore. You have to try and lose him in the darkness.

GO TO 60.

'Julian?' you ask. 'Who the hell is Julian?'

'I have literally no idea, mate,' Joe replies. 'I've never heard of a Julian to do with this place.' He looks down at the board and asks the only one who might know. 'Who's Julian?'

The glass moves. D. E. A. T. H.

'I don't like this,' you say, 'we should stop now.'

'Stop?' Joe says, shocked. 'How can we stop while this is happening? This is amazing! This is the proof we've been trying to find all this time. They're talking! Someone's finally, definitely, talking!'

'And listen to what they're saying,' you reply. The glass moves again. D. A. N. G. E. R. G. O.

'You want to argue with them?' you ask. 'Because I sure as hell don't. If this is genuine…'

'Of course it's genuine,' says Joe, 'I'm not moving the glass. Are you moving the glass?'

'You know I'm not,' you tell him.

The glass moves to the words GOOD BYE and stays there.

'Hello?' says Joe, his voice loud, echoing slightly around the room. 'Are you still there?'

The glass stays still. You lift your fingers off it. 'Come on.'

'You shouldn't just do that,' he tells you. 'You shouldn't just break the connection.'

'I didn't,' you reply, '*it* did.' You're trying to stay calm but if this is real – and you know it is really, deep down you *know* – then the dead have been talking to you. And they're telling you to get out. Only an idiot argues with the dead. 'It told us to go. So we should go.' You pause for a second, waiting for Joe to say something. Then, louder, exasperated, 'Shouldn't we?'

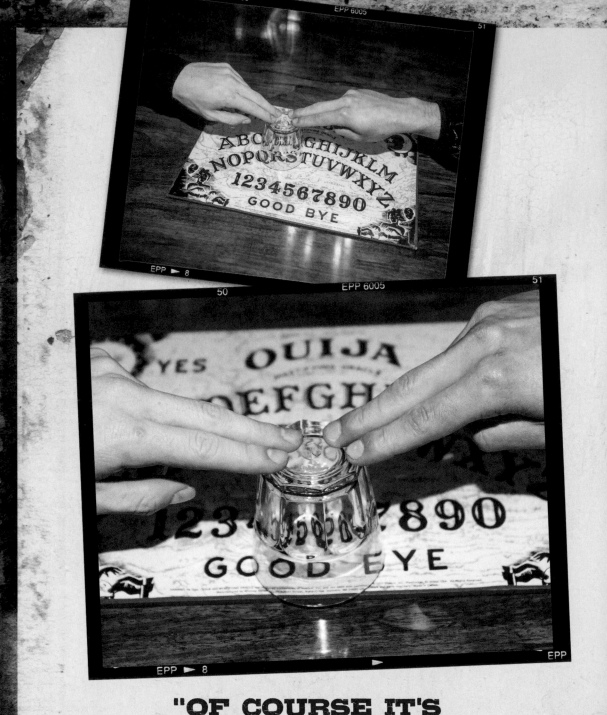

"OF COURSE IT'S GENUINE. I'M NOT MOVING THE GLASS"

Joe nods. 'Yeah, I guess we should. Of course we should.'

Between the two of you, you quickly pack up the Ouija board and glass and grab the cameras.

You head back to the lift. You're not that excited about getting back in it, the fact you got away with it the first time is beginning to feel like a lucky break but it's the quickest way out of here and that's the deciding factor.

Joe presses the call button and the lift doors open. You get in, the doors close behind you and Joe presses the button for the ground floor.

'Can you believe that actually happened?' Joe asks. 'Before there's always been a chance that it was fake, you know? That someone was pushing the glass. But I seriously wasn't doing that. My fingers were barely touching it.'

'Neither were mine,' you agree, 'and it was terrifying.'

'And we got it on film!'

The lift starts moving with a heavy clunk.

'It's going to be the best video yet,' you say, 'no doubt about it.'

And you can't wait to be back in your house, with all the lights on, watching it, knowing you experienced it but got out of there.

The lift stops. Why has the lift stopped?

'What's happening?' you ask, even though you know Joe has no more idea than you do.

He looks through the frosted glass of the lift door. 'I think we're between two floors,' he says, 'it's hard to tell but with the way the light is coming through there,' he points at a dark band at the bottom of the glass, 'that looks like the ground,' he shifts his finger to the lighter section above it, 'and that's the floor above it.'

You look at the indicator but nothing's illuminated. 'We could be between the second and third floors then.' This is just ridiculous. Please don't say you're now going to be stuck in the damn thing?

Suddenly, the glass panel in the door shatters and being stuck is the last thing on your mind.

'What the hell?' shouts Joe, falling back as you're both showered with the broken glass.

In the space where the window used to be you see a pair of feet.

'There's someone out there!' you cry.

And then a long blade just misses your face.

'Fuck!' Joe shouts as the blade swings about inside the lift. Both of you drop to the ground on instinct and now you can see what it is. It's a pikestaff, like the one you saw earlier next to the suit of armour. The long blade has a barbed hook at its base, and, just for a second you imagine you and Joe like a pair of fish trapped in this dry tank, just waiting for that hook to snag you – tearing, gouging into you – so that whoever is on the other end of this thing can yank you out.

They can't see you clearly, that much is obvious from the way the blade swings about inside the lift. If the lift had stopped any higher you would be dead, whoever this is could have just stabbed you. As it is they're aiming blind, poking and swinging and thrusting, just hoping they can catch one of you.

Both of you press yourselves against the front of the lift. If you stay there and keep low, you're out of reach of the pikestaff. But you can't stay there forever?

Joe makes a grab for the pikestaff but whoever is swinging it is moving it too quickly, too randomly; Joe snatches his hands away before he loses some fingers.

'Do you think we can get the door open?' he asks, turning and trying to get his fingers into the gap between the door and the wall of the lift. 'If we can do that we might be able to jump out onto the second floor.'

It's got to be worth a try. The two of you claw at the edge of the door, trying to get a grip on it.

'I think I've got it,' you tell him, your fingers slowly forcing themselves into the gap. The door shifts a tiny amount and now you've definitely a good grip, Joe too. The two of you pull as hard as you can, the mechanism of the door fighting you back. Just above you, the blade of the pikestaff is still swinging and it actually clips you slightly on the top of your head as you shift position to give yourself more leverage. It's not serious, though you can feel a slight trickle of blood going down the back of your neck.

The door suddenly gives, shifting halfway open before stopping again. It yanks the pikestaff with it and, for a second you hope you might even have knocked it from the grip of whoever is holding it. Then it starts thrusting again, your attacker has obviously lifted the pole up as high as they can and is now just stabbing it down in your direction. Luckily, with the pole angled against the floor above, they still can't get you.

'Once more,' says Joe and, with a roar, both of you pull at the door. For a second you think it's not going to move but then there's a tearing of gears and it slams back in place. Behind you, the blade of the pikestaff stabs into the wall of the lift, the door pulling it right over to one side.

You pull the concertina door half open and the two of you jump down to the second floor. Behind you, you can hear whoever it was that was attacking you pull the pikestaff free.

As you roll on the ground you can hear running feet from the floor above. Your attacker is now running for the stairs.

But so are you and Joe.

And then you remember. Standing there looking down the stairs as the feet get closer above.

'We can't get past,' says Joe, 'the stairs are battered on this floor.'

He's right of course, halfway down there's nothing but torn and splintered wood.

Above, turning the corner you see the man who tried to kill you in the lift. He's holding the pikestaff and he's grinning. If it weren't for the weapon in his hands you wouldn't be scared of him. He's in his early twenties, thin and wearing tracksuit bottoms and a hoodie.

'Hello,' he says, 'want to start running yet?'

'Who the hell are you?' Joe asks.

'Mooney maybe?' he says.

'Mooney?' Joe relaxes slightly and turns to you. 'You know I said there was a bloke at the bank who was a fan of the videos, the bloke that gave us the keys?'

'Yeah,' you say.

'This is him,' says Joe. He looks at Mooney. 'What are you playing at man? You scared the shit out of us.'

'Have you talked to her?' he asks, then grins, 'I know you have, so don't lie.'

'Talked to who?' Joe asks.

'Katy,' he says. 'Sad, so, so sad…'

'I have no idea what you're talking about, mate,' says Joe. But you're starting to think you might.

'She must have mentioned me,' Mooney says, starting to come down the stairs. 'She wouldn't have called me Mooney, that's just my username. She'd have called me Julian.'

'Oh shit,' Joe whispers, and you're inclined to agree with him.

GO TO 35.

54

'H e drowned in there?' you ask, looking towards the pond. 'Surely it's not that deep?'

'Everyone was so distracted by the fire that Toby Hurrell's body wasn't discovered until much later. They kept searching the building for him and then, finally, one of the insurance people came out here and found him floating face down right in the middle of the pond.'

'Poor guy.'

'The fish had eaten away most of his face.'

Suddenly there's a splash from the pond.

'Jesus!' Joe shouts, and turns his camera at the water.

'What the hell was that?' you ask.

'I don't know. Something flew through the air, a stone or something.' He moves to the side of the pool. The water is rippling, sending the scum islands and the reflected moonlight in waves across the surface.

'You think someone's lobbing stuff at us?'

'I…' he's unsure, 'maybe. From where though?'

You look towards the hotel. 'From one of the windows, maybe?'

'Hell of a throw, possible though I suppose.'

'I don't like this mate,' you say, 'this is genuinely sketchy. First the lights, then that guy running off, now someone throwing stuff at us.'

'Yeah,' he says, 'I know what you mean. You want to leave?'

'I don't know.' You sort of do if you're honest but, at the same time, leaving now – and never being able to come back – that doesn't sit right. 'What do you think?'

'I think I want to run back to the car and get out of here,' he says, 'but if we do that we've got nothing have we? We haven't even set foot in the building yet.'

'No.' He's having the same problem as you. Running away just feels… such a waste. 'Let's keep going but be careful, you know?'

'Seriously,' he replies, 'one more bit of freaky shit and you're going to be chasing me down that drive because I'm out of here.'

GO TO 30.

It's a big function room with rows of seats set out for an audience. Some of the chairs have tipped over and you can imagine the audience, on hearing the fire alarm, running for the exit. At the far end there's a small stage with a table on it, four chairs set behind it.

A sign on a stand, just inside the door, says 'Eaten Alive! – The History of Cannibals in Horror Cinema'.

'Sounds tasty,' you reply, moving towards the stage area at the far end while Joe explores a cupboard set into the wall by the door.

'There's loads of kit in here,' he says, 'AV stuff. I can see why they locked the place up.'

You climb up onto the stage and look at the stuff scattered on the table. Sheets of notes from whoever had been on this panel. You pick one up. '"Italian gut munchers,"'you read out.

'Italian what now?' Joe asks from the other end of the room.

'No idea,' you reply, scanning through the rest of the notes. A load of movie titles and names of directors and actors, you guess. You put the notes back down and pick up what looks like a souvenir booklet for the convention. A rotting corpse lifts itself out of a grave, holding up a banner that says 'HorrorTime' on it, the letters written in a font that looks like dripping blood. You start to flick through it but all of a sudden a bright beam of light strikes out across the room and a scream fills the air, the sort of desperate, throat-ripping scream that can only come from someone who knows they're about to die. In shock, you drop the booklet to the floor and stagger back against the curtains that line the back of the stage. Blinded by the light, your foot teeters on the lip of the raised edge. The scream fades and now the air is filled with the angry whine of a chainsaw. You have no idea what's happening as you fall backwards, hands raised against the light and

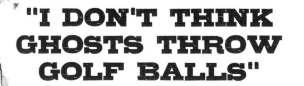

"I DON'T THINK
GHOSTS THROW
GOLF BALLS"

shattered by a zombie hand reaching out through it. You look inside the bag, it's mostly flyers and sheets of paper listing the different panels that were being held. '"You Check In But You Don't Check Out!"' you read out to Joe, '"The Haunted Hotel in Horror Fiction."'

'They should have just told the guests to walk around the place,' he says. 'It's all right here.'

Suddenly, there's the sound of smashing glass as something comes flying through the window.

'Christ!' Joe drops to the floor while you dart inside the bathroom door, both of you looking at the window and the brand new hole right in the middle of one of the panes.

'What the hell was that?' you ask.

Joe shuffles along the floor and picks up a golf ball. He holds it up so you can see it.

'Seriously?' you ask. 'Someone's lobbing golf balls at us?'

'Seems that way,' he says.

He inches towards the window, keeping as low as he can then shines his torch out. 'Probably just kids messing about,' he suggests.

'I hope so!' You step back out of the bathroom, sticking close to the wall and joining him at the window.

'I don't think ghosts throw golf balls about,' he says.

'Poltergeists,' you say.

'Tiger Woods da Poltergeist?'

You roll your eyes. 'They throw things around.'

He's grinning. 'I know, I know… Help me open the window, mate,' he says.

'Why?'

'Because I want to give them their ball back.'

He stands up on one side of the window while you're at the other. You both reach out to grab the frame so you can slide the window up without having to stand right in front of it.

You both listen. There's no noise from outside.

'Probably run off,' Joe says, 'but just in case.'

He throws the ball as hard as he can out into the night. There's silence for a couple of seconds and then you hear a low splash.

'I think you got it into the pond,' you say.

'Hope I didn't K.O. a fish,' he replies. 'Let's see if we can find another open room.'

You dash out of there before another ball can come flying in and move further along the corridor.

The rest of the doors are all locked shut.

'Well, this sucks,' you say.

'We'll have to try another floor I guess,' Joe suggests and you both move towards the main stairs. 'They look safe enough,' he says, looking up at the flight that leads to the top floor. Soot is streaked in huge bands across the walls and the carpet is burned down to stubble, crisp to the touch.

You look down and you can just see the damage below. 'Maybe we should take the backstairs,' you suggest, 'I really don't want to die, y'see. I'm funny like that.'

He takes the first couple of steps up, slamming his feet down. 'They're solid, don't worry, nobody's dying on the stairs tonight.'

GO TO 31.

58

You enter the room and it's filled with moonlight. The ceiling and three of the walls are made entirely from glass, designed to look out over the area around the hotel. There's a table in the window and a few easy chairs dotted around the room. In the far corner what you assume is a bar is sealed away behind its metal shutter.

'This place is amazing,' you say, moving over to one of the large picture windows.

Joe makes to flick the lights on but you tell him to leave it. 'Once they're on we won't be able to see outside.'

'Fair enough,' he agrees, moving his hand away from the switches and coming over to join you at the windows.

'Imagine a telescope set up in here,' you say as you look out, 'you can see for miles.'

'Maybe that's what it used to be, an observatory or something,' Joe suggests.

As your eyes get used to the darkness you can see more and more of the world outside. The moon and starlight turning it into a patchwork of black trees and grey open fields. In the distance you can see the village, with only a few lights left burning in the windows of the buildings. It's late, most of its residents will have gone to bed.

'This is as good a place as any to try something,' suggests Joe, pulling the rucksack from his back, opening it and pulling out the Ouija board.

'I might have known that would come out sooner or later,' you say with a smile that you hope will look more confident in the dim light than it actually is.

'You up for it?' he asks.

'I suppose,' you agree.

Joe sets the Ouija board on the table, and places a small glass on top of it.

'We'll need a little light to film,' says Joe as he gets the tripods out of his rucksack and sets one camera up on each side of the table.

He moves over to the light switches to experiment with them. One turns on a few concealed lights around the room. It's a bit brighter but not so bright you're killing the atmosphere.

'Perfect,' Joe says, sitting down on one of the chairs. 'Come on then. Let's see who's out there.'

You sit down on the chair next to him and both of you reach out to place your fingers on the glass.

GO TO 22.

"THIS IS AS GOOD A PLACE AS ANY TO TRY SOMETHING."

James Mallahan was of the opinion that hotels were a luxury. This was because he could never afford to stay in them. So when he did manage to do it – the one advantage to working in medical supplies was that, every now and then, they paid to shove you on a course, a free holiday slightly ruined by boring bits – he made the most of it.

The room was very nice, filled with the sort of furniture his flat wasn't. A big old bed with nice sheets and blankets – nobody had blankets at home anymore did they? It was all duvets and flat pillows – and a shower that was so powerful getting clean was an adventure. A boxing match against high water-pressure.

There was a movie on the film channel he'd fancied seeing for ages.

He had his night planned. He'd told the people on the course that he wouldn't be able to see them this evening because he had some work to do. ('I know,' he'd sighed theatrically, rolling his eyes, '*so* boring.') He wouldn't even make it to dinner. They'd commiserated and said they'd make up for it the next night.

It was all a lie. James had his eye on lots of naughty food from room service, including a bottle of red wine, and a brilliantly lazy night sat in his pants on the bed watching Will Smith shoot some people.

Bliss.

He rang down his food order. (Do I want extra garlic bread? Oh why not.) He turned the TV on and waited for all the happy to kick in.

Which is when the noises started coming from the bathroom sink.

They were strange noises, somewhere between someone trying to unblock a drain and a horse being beaten to death with a hammer.

He peered down the plughole – pointless but what else could you do? – and wondered if he was going to have to call someone to look at it. A bored night manager making banging noises in his bathroom wasn't half going to take the edge of his evening though wasn't it? Maybe he could just close the door and worry about it in the…

The hand came bursting out of the plughole and grabbed him by the hair.

'Help me!' a voice screamed. 'He's trying to kill me!'

'You and me both,' he thought briefly before all of his calm resolve burst and he started screaming and kicking at the sink.

The night porter found him sitting on the closed lid of the toilet twenty minutes later, sobbing and staring at the sink – which exhibited no sign of strange behaviour as far as the porter could tell.

Debra Wilkinson really had no time for all this pretence. Honestly, it was a grubby old house pretending to be something special. I mean, seriously, suits of armour? Oil paintings of dead peers? Where did they get all this crap? There was probably a really sad IKEA just for miserable hotels, filled to the rafters with hokey old tat that would appeal to American tourists.

And draughts? It was quite absurd, it wasn't just that there was a couple, it was more a case of there being nowhere in her room where she could sit without having a northern wind set her teeth chattering.

They should just knock the whole place down and replace it with something fit for purpose. She told her sister as much on the phone while pacing around her room trying to find a warm spot.

'It's just hopeless, darling,' she said, 'I think I've booked into Guantanamo Bay by accident. If you never hear from me again, assume I died from food poisoning. Or hypothermia. Or boredom.'

Those words would come back to haunt her that night when she was woken in the early hours of the morning by a hand clutching at her throat. She came to in a panic, opened her mouth to scream but the pillow suddenly, roughly, shoved against her face made that quite impossible. She tried to kick out, but her attacker – could there really be only one, how many pairs of hands were coming for her in the dark – seemed to be tying her legs together. Her hands too, pulled either side of the bed so firmly she felt the muscles in her shoulders threaten to tear. She was quite convinced she would be dead within a few minutes but then, miraculously, she found herself free. She scooted up the bed and slammed her hand on the light switch. She couldn't begin to understand how the room was empty. It couldn't be. The door hadn't opened (not that anyone would have had time to run out anyway) so where was her attacker? Looking down at the bed, the sheets rolled into thick strips she had a sudden idea, but immediately dismissed it. Debra Wilkinson was a sensible woman and beds simply didn't come to life and attack the people sleeping in them.

Did they?

'The bed,' Simon Kirby thought, 'it's under the bed.'

He'd first heard the noise about five minutes ago. It had woken him up and he hadn't had the first idea what it could be. It sounded like someone dragging themselves around on the floor but that was silly. There was nobody else here after all. The noise must be coming from outside.

But it wasn't. As his sleepy mind fully woke it was clear that it wasn't. It was coming from inside the room and it was moving towards him. A slow, dragging sound with an extra creak to it – the creaking immediately made him picture a body hanging from a noose, which didn't help his nerves. What was it?

It got closer and closer and he slowly reached for the light switch. He hesitated. On the one hand he wanted to know what was making that noise. (Was that breathing, heavy tortured breathing?) On the other hand he *really* didn't.

Simon turned on the light and nearly managed to convince himself that he hadn't just seen a dirty, wrinkled foot vanish under the corner of the bed.

Nearly.

'I should look,' he thought, 'I have to. It's not as if I can just lie here while that – whatever it is – stays under there. I have to look. I have to know.'

Or he could run for it. Only an idiot would shift onto his knees, lower his head and peer under there. He wasn't a child after all, it's not like the days when he had lain in bed at night convinced there was something beneath him, sure that if he were to let a single part of him leave the safety of the duvet it would grab him. No. He would leap out of bed, run towards the door and then stop, turn and look.

On three. One… two… three!

He jumped out of bed and he could hear the thing moving. Sliding out from the shadows and coming for him! How could it move so quickly? He reached for the door, determined not to look, determined not to turn around. Determined…

He looked.

Simon woke the whole floor up as he ran screaming along the corridor a few seconds later.

GO BACK TO 30.

You run into the maze, beating at the overgrown branches that lash out at you as you pass.

Your eyes are adjusting to the moonlight and you can just about see your way as you take paths at random. You've got a slight lead on Julian now, this is your chance.

You stop running, moving your hands along the foliage of the hedge. What you need to do is… yes! There!

You force yourself into the hedge, trying to move as quietly as possible, hiding yourself inside it. You're hunched at a ridiculous angle, and your neck is immediately aching from the position you've forced it into. That's OK, you won't have to stand like this for long.

You can hear Julian coming.

'Stop running!' he shouts. 'Come back here!'

'Yeah right,' you think, 'of course I will mate, sorry to put you to all this trouble.'

He's in the path to your right. If he follows the route you took – and you really hope he does – he'll walk on another few metres and then turn into the path on his left, then he'll walk past the place where you forced yourself in here. And once he's done that, once he's got a little way ahead, you can climb out and run back to the hotel.

He stops running.

'You can't get out of here!' he shouts. 'Not without the key.'

Silence. You're holding as still as you can, knowing that one move could tell him where you are.

'Come out!' he screams, and shoves the pikestaff into the hedge. The blade misses you by only a few centimetres and your immediate instinct is to climb out and run as fast as you can. But you stay still, because that was just coincidence wasn't it? He doesn't actually know you're there. He just stabbed at the hedge in frustration, not knowing how close he could have come to killing you.

He pulls the pikestaff back out, the barbed hook catching on the foliage and shaking the whole hedge. You take the opportunity to adjust your position, getting at a better angle to be able to climb back out and run when – *if* – he goes past.

The pikestaff comes free and Julian shouts again. No words this time just a childlike roar of frustration. You've never heard someone sound so utterly, utterly insane.

Then he starts moving again, and the plan is working because he takes the left path. Now you just have to hope that he can't see where you've displaced the branches climbing in here. You're pretty sure you're hidden, you've burrowed as deeply into the hedge as you can without sticking out the other side.

He walks towards you. Stops again. Makes a low growling sound in his throat.

Then walks right past you. It worked!

Now to wait as long as you dare, let him get ahead.

He gets to the end of this path and turns right, moving deeper into the maze. Slowly, as quietly as you can, you pull yourself out and back onto the path. You stop for a second and listen to the sound of Julian walking away. He stops. Then starts heading back in the direction he's just come! Back towards you! Do you climb back into the hedge or just make a run for it?

You run, and it might have been OK if it wasn't for the overgrown branch that scratches at your face as you pass. The shocked cry is out of your mouth before you can stop it and, behind you, Julian laughs.

'I can hear you!' he calls and starts running again.

You've gained some ground at least, if you can keep up the pace you should be able to get back to the hotel before he does. Get back to Joe.

The exit of the maze is just ahead, you can see where the hedge walls open out once more, the partially lit hotel in the distance. Yes. You're going to make this.

Then something catches your legs and you go flying through the air.

Landing painfully on the grass, you grab at the thing that tangled in your legs and tripped you. It's a golf club, a putter, they must have a putting green here and someone left this one lying around. Of all the shitty luck!

Maybe you can use it as a weapon though, because Julian has turned around the last corner of the maze and is running towards you, that pikestaff pointing right at your head.

You get to your knees, taking a firm grip on the club and swing it out in a wide arc as he closes in. You knock the pikestaff aside but Julian kicks out at you, his shoe jarring off the side of your face, knocking you flat on your back and making your head swim. It's no good, you'll never get to your feet in time, he won't let you. He's screaming and raising the pikestaff to stab it right down and into your chest. This is it. It's all over.

'Stop!' Joe shouts and all of a sudden you're bathed in light from one of the cameras.

Julian pauses, both of you looking over towards the source of the light as Joe walks towards you. His face is lit by his phone screen and you can see a trickle of blood running down his cheek. It looks completely black in the half-light.

'You do not want to do that, Julian,' he shouts.

'Are you…' Julian peers against the light, 'are you actually filming still? Even now? You're like those idiots in found-footage movies, still waving their cameras around when they should just be running. Nobody's going to see your stupid little video!' he screams.

'They're seeing it right now,' says Joe. He's stood right by you both now, the phone and the camera held out in front of him like a crucifix to a vampire. 'We're live streaming mate,' he says, glancing at the screen, 'nine thousand and forty three people currently watching. Seeing every stupid move you make.'

This throws Julian. To be honest it throws you a bit too.

'I don't believe you,' Julian says finally. But you can tell from his face he's not as convinced of that as he might like to pretend.

'Amazing15, currently online, says this is my best video yet,' says Joe, reading from the screen, 'he's also called the police. So have I of course, so have lots of people watching.' He glances back at the screen. 'McGill94 says "That guy is so screwed!" Ha!' Joe grins. 'They're certainly not wrong.'

'Put it down!' Julian screams, now pointing the pikestaff towards Joe. You take the opportunity to scrabble further away from him and get to your feet.

'Now why would he do that?' you say. 'While he's pointing the phone at you, you can't do a thing. Face it mate, you *are* screwed.'

Julian roars again, stabbing at the grass with the pikestaff. He looks like an angry toddler, desperate to get his own way.

'Your only chance,' Joe says, 'is to run. You probably won't get far but,' he shrugs, 'what else can you do?'

Julian stares at you both for another couple of seconds and then bolts.

GO TO 62.

'I don't care,' you say, 'I'm sorry but I really don't. There's no way I'm carrying on with that. It's…' You really don't want to say the word 'evil' because it sounds stupid. It would make you sound like a character in a shitty old horror movie with bad dialogue. But it's the word that sticks in your head nonetheless. Sitting there, being in touch with… spirits, that's how Joe would put it but let's be honest, let's call them what they are: the dead. That's who you're talking to. Dead people. Dead people screaming.

This was supposed to be fun. Scary maybe, but only in a good way. A fun way. Exciting, thrilling, brushing against the unknown. There's a huge difference between that and staring horror in the face as it stares right back. As it speaks to you. As it *screams* at you.

Joe shakes his head, disappointed. 'They're spirits,' he says. 'They can't harm us!'

He's changing his story already, you think. A minute ago you were in danger if you stopped talking to them, now they can't harm you anyway. So which is it? You just don't care anymore. You want to leave, you want to get out of this building and get back to the car. You want to be driving away from here, going back to a life that's nice and normal and sane and where the dead shut up.

You look out of the window at the darkness outside. It's harder to see now, because of the lights you've turned on, there's a reflection of Joe hanging there like a ghost in the glass.

Ghost in the glass. Yeah.

Is that all it is? The more you look, the more it seems to you that it's actually getting darker out there.

You look up at the sky, where the moon and the stars are bright enough to still be visible despite the reflected light. One by one the stars seem to be going out, like blown bulbs. A wave of something – clouds, it must be clouds – moving across the night sky and snuffing out the light. The moon is the last to vanish but when it does it's only your reflection that makes the window look like anything more than a wall painted black.

You stare at your own face, and then glance over at Joe who's still sat in the chair, head down. He's probably trying to think of what he can say that might manage to convince you. Well tough, there's nothing he can say, you've made up your mind, you're getting out of here.

Then, in the reflection, you see the door to the room opening slowly and, panicking, you turn to see who's coming in. But the door in the real world – the solid world not the reflection – *hasn't moved.* It's still closed.

You look back at the reflection and now there's a figure in the open doorway, silhouetted against the light from the corridor beyond. It's a thin man and he's walking into the room, walking towards *you.*

You turn to look over your shoulder again. There's nobody there.

'Joe,' you whisper. 'Come here.'

'What is it?' he asks.

'Just come here!' You're hissing the words, not daring to raise your voice, because the man in the reflection is getting closer now. He's stepping into the halo of one of the lights and you catch a glimpse of part of his face. He's old, his nose long and hooked. Is he smiling?

Joe walks over to join you. He moves slowly, dejected because you won't continue.

'Look.' You point at the reflection, being careful not to let your finger touch the glass. Part of you thinks that if you touched the glass your finger would just pass through, as if you were sticking it into thick liquid.

Joe looks. 'What?'

'You can't see that?' you ask.

'See what?'

The man is now halfway across the room, he's coming right up behind you and Joe. And of course, you know who it is. You've seen that face before haven't you? It's Isaac Godling. The man who brought all the horror to this building – or if he didn't bring it, he certainly built on it – and now he's coming for you.

'The reflection,' you tell him, 'look at the reflection.'

Joe stares at the glass and you can tell by the look on his face that he can't see it because if he did he'd be looking more scared. He'd be looking like you.

Again, you look over your shoulder at the empty room, you can't help it, you have to, because Isaac is now only a short distance away and he's extending his right arm. A single pointed finger raised towards you. Is he pointing at you? At Joe? Is he reaching out to tap you on the shoulder?

You look back at the reflection because, as much as you don't want to see him, the idea of not knowing where he is is even worse.

His finger reaches out, closer and closer but he's not reaching out to you, he's reaching out to the glass, because somehow he's not in the room, he's on the other side of the window, in that other world, the world that lies just alongside this one, the world where the dead live.

His finger comes closer. You're shaking now. You can't look away. You have a feeling you know what will happen when that finger touches the glass, the *barrier*, the wall between this world and his.

Closer and closer.

The finger touches.

The sound of breaking glass, the room filling with glistening shards, briefly reflecting the moonlight before, like hundreds of tiny knives flying right at you, they cut and tear and kill. You scream, but not for long..

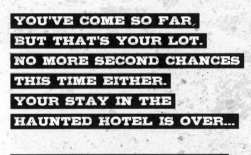

YOU'VE COME SO FAR, BUT THAT'S YOUR LOT. NO MORE SECOND CHANCES THIS TIME EITHER. YOUR STAY IN THE HAUNTED HOTEL IS OVER...

UNTIL YOU START AGAIN.

62

Julian runs. Of course he does. He has no choice.

He's aiming for the gate, get through that and his car's only a short way down the driveway. Once he's behind the wheel the police will have a job catching up. 'And then what?' says Katy's voice in his head, 'You keep running? They'll find you, Julian, and so will I.'

He reaches the gate and digs in his pocket for the keys. They're not there. How can they not be there?

He has a sudden mental image of emptying his pockets on the desk in the upstairs room he's been sitting in all night. Habit really, taking out his wallet, keys, loose change, dumping them on the desk like he always does so he can sit comfortably. How stupid was that? Now he can't get out!

But he has to. He starts trying to climb the gate but he can't get a grip, the chain-link wire is too narrow, he just can't get a purchase on it with his feet.

The wall, it'll have to be the wall.

He looks up at it, staring at the bales of barbed wire on the top. He'll manage, he'll have to. If he's careful, he should be able to get over it.

He starts to climb. The wall is easy enough, the old bricks are full of holes for his hands and feet. Once he's at the top, he carefully pushes himself through the barbed wire, ducking under one strand, poking his leg past another. If he takes it slowly, carefully, he can do this, it's very loosely wound.

'Julian?' He snaps his head around in panic at the sound of her voice and that's all it takes, he loses his balance and falls down on the outside of the wall, a loop of barbed wire snagging at his throat.

He wants to scream but the sound is choked from him as the weight of his body pulls the wire taut and he ends up hanging there, his back against the wall, the wire like a noose around his throat. A wet, tearing noose, spilling his blood in great gushes.

He's not alone. He can see Katy now, walking towards him, her wet, puffy feet making no sound as she steps through the undergrowth.

'Clumsy,' she says, with a smile.

Her friends are with her. The woman whose head burns, the flesh spitting and burning in the heat, a roman candle in a business suit. The smartly dressed man, his suit jacket draped with pondweed, his face barely more than holes where the bone smiles through.

More and more of them appear from between the trees. The dead of Priory Grange come to welcome him to their club.

And here, of course, is the old man. Isaac Godling, with a smile that reflects the moon.

'So good of you to join us,' he says, and as Julian's vision begins to fade from asphyxiation and blood loss, he can feel the hands of the dead pulling him closer, welcoming him to his new home.

GO TO 68.

'Yeah,' Joe agrees, 'let's keep looking around.'

The corridor stretches to either side of the stairs. You aim left and walk along past more locked rooms. A lot of the lights are out in the corridor, but there doesn't seem to be much to see. Please don't say you walked up here for nothing.

'Look.' Joe, says, shining his torch at a pair of double doors. Next to the doors is a sign saying 'Roof Lounge'.

'Let's take a look,' you say.

GO TO 58.

65

You just want to get out of there so you head straight for the exit. You run across the forecourt, kicking up gravel as you try to push yourself even faster.

You've still got the camera in your hand. For a second, you wish it was something bigger and heavier, something you might actually be able to defend yourself with but at least it has a light, and without that you'd probably trip over the buried pieces of the old fountain, or run right into the open arms of the stone angel.

You don't want to look over your shoulder because that'll only slow you down but you can hear Julian getting closer. Bloody hell he's fast. You're a good runner but he's getting closer, you're sure of it, maybe when you're as mad as he is it gives you an advantage. You're on the driveway now, and nearly out of the place, maybe you'll be able to lose him in the woods?

You see the gate ahead of you and that's when you realise you've made a mistake. It's locked. Of course it's locked. Joe has the keys in his pocket. No doubt Julian has a set too; he wouldn't have been able to get in here otherwise. Somehow you doubt he's going to let you borrow them.

You look to the wall on either side, with its bales of barbed wire and you know for sure you're not risking that. Even if you could climb the wall, you'd tear yourself to pieces trying to get over.

It's too late to turn around and go back, the driveway isn't wide enough, Julian will be able to stop you. You've only got one choice: try and climb the gate.

You take a run at it, leaping up and grabbing the wire, scrabbling with your feet, trying to get purchase. It's no good, the chain-link is too narrow and you end up dangling by your fingers, the sound of Julian's feet getting closer and closer on the gravel behind you.

A low buzzing begins to sound from inside the fuse box.

'That's not a good noise,' you say, flipping the cover back and stepping down from the table.

'What did you do?' Joe asks.

'Absolutely nothing,' you tell him.

The buzzing sound is getting louder.

'So what's that sound then?' asks Joe. 'You think it's short-circuiting or something?'

'I have no idea.'

The hum suddenly surges in volume, the lights flashing on, just for a second.

'Mate, you think something could be about to blow?' Joe asks. 'I do not want to be stood here when this place decides to burst into flames again.'

Another surge of buzzing, another flash of the lights and this time you're sure you saw something move in that brief moment when the room was lit.

'Shine your light over towards the stairs,' you tell Joe.

'Why?'

You're now both pointing your cameras into the room but there's nothing there.

'I could have sworn…' you begin but then the light flashes again and there's no doubt this time. There's a figure stood by the base of the stairs. 'You see that?' you ask Joe, the room now pitch black again.

'See what?'

You're pointing your camera at the spot where you know you saw the figure. A man, lit up just for an instant. 'There was a guy stood there,' you explain, 'right by the stairs.'

The lights return. Again it's only for a brief moment, only as long as a camera flash, a pulse of light and then back to darkness. But in that moment you see the man again except this time he isn't alone, there's another figure a few feet away, a woman, her hair long and dirty, her arms wrapped around her in a straightjacket.

So why can't you see them in the camera's light? Because when you pan the camera over the spot where you know the figures were stood, there's nothing there.

'I saw him,' says Joe. 'Old geeza, big nose, grey hair…'

'Right?' and you know you're shouting, because this is scaring the hell out of you and you can't keep your voice steady. 'So why can't we see him with camera lights?'

'We need to get out of here,' Joe says, and you don't even waste time agreeing with him, you both turn back towards the main door.

Then the lights snap back on for one last time. You glance behind and see the man and woman right behind you. The man's arms are outstretched, the woman's mouth is opening impossibly wide, lips stretching, mouth distending, like a python dislocating its jaw so it can swallow a goat.

Then it's dark again and you can't see anything anymore, you just feel the man's hands tightening around your throat, skin crumbling and flaking, finger bones cracking. You hear Joe scream but it's immediately muffled and you imagine that impossibly large mouth closing over him. There's a wet, crunching, chewing sound in the darkness and you're trying to pull the fingers from your throat but you can't feel them with your hands, just on your neck where they tighten and tighten and…

OK, so now you've learned something. The choices you make don't always work out well. This building is dangerous. Forget what you believe is possible. Forget the rules. You might not get out of here alive. So watch your step, choose carefully and maybe you'll live through this.

NOW GO TO 28, AND CHOOSE MORE CAREFULLY IN FUTURE.

You're both sitting on the front steps of the hotel, waiting. The police should be here any minute.

'I'm not looking forward to explaining this, mate,' you say. 'I mean... are they going to think we did it? That we killed him?'

Joe shakes his head and pats the camera and the phones. 'I reckon we've got enough evidence here to cover ourselves on that, don't you? And then we've got the viewers – there'll end up being a couple of million witnesses backing us too – we'll be good.'

'Yeah.'

You think you can hear the sirens now, the cars heading up the country road you and Joe drove along earlier.

'What a night,' Joe says.

You nod. 'I wish it had gone differently that's for sure.'

'That's life,' he says. 'You can't go back over your decisions, you just have to stick with them. Ask Julian, he's proof of that.'

But you can go back, can't you? Because every decision offers you a different route. So, why give up now?

GO TO 1, AND START AGAIN.

IF YOU DARE.

ACKNOWLEDGEMENTS

Ghost-written by Joe Weller...

Even though it's normally just myself and Elliot left to fend for ourselves in my videos, there's no way this book, the tour and promotion could have happened, to such a high standard, without my good friends at Headline Publishing. They really did take a big risk on me but I am so thankful for the opportunity and how brilliantly they and Guy Adams have helped bring my crazy idea to life!

Also shout out to my main gangstas at OP Talent, who continue to bring more exciting and mental opportunities my way.

Thank you, Elliot Crawford, for pushing me to go into the first ever haunted abandoned building I'd been in. Thank you, Harry Lee-Preston, for helping me to develop my exploring skills, become mentally tougher and dominate whatever obstacle is in front of me.

Most importantly, to every single person that supports me doing what I enjoy, thank you.